COVID Confinement, Or Much A Flu About Muffin

By Gregory John Ferris

Also by Gregory John Ferris

La Famille Bilingue and A Simply Nothing

Zoe : An Act in Two Plays
          La Lisière De La Forêt (Treeline)
          Only Stupid Birds Sing

One Hundred and Sixty Four Buttons

Inutile

The author would like to thank Anne Harlan for her support of the Alliance Française of Louisville

MUFFIN BUTTON	Widowed, rich aunt of the Button family
DAMON BUTTON	Muffin's nephew, free lance writer
AMY BUTTON	Wife of Damon, former nurse
SAWYER BUTTON	Teenage son of Amy and Damon
KYLIE	20 year old neighbor, Sawyer's friend
DORIS TIPTON	Damon's editor (via Zoom)
MASON RIDLEY	Damon's cousin (voice only)

SETTING

The Button home in Louisville, Kentucky
Spring 2020
All scenes take place in the Button living room

Act I scene 1 Mid morning
Act I scene 2 30 minutes later
Act I scene 3 Several days later
Act I scene 4   Three days later
Act I scene 5   A week later

Act II scene 1 Two days later
Act II scene 2 The same day, late at night
Act II scene 3 Three days later

SCENE 1

(Lying on a desk, a cell phone rings, Damon, seated, reaches to answer it, on speaker, while he regards his computer screen. He is unshaven and wearing aound the home mismatched clothes).

DAMON

Hey Mason.

MASON

Hi Damon. Are you at home ?

DAMON

Where else would I be ? I can only take so much of Krogers. If I spend two more hours there this week, I will be in their union automatically.

MASON

Aunt Muffin isn't home.

DAMON

Are you conducting a census of which family members are home and which aren't. Mark me down as chez moi.

Or, is that your way of telling me that she died ? I hadn ;t heard. Was it COVID ?

No, if had been, we'd have heard that she was sick. Good news travels quickly. Not suicide again ?

MASON

Suicide again ? Are you drinking already ? What the heck is suicide again .

DAMON

The last time she was rumored to have died, I suspected suicide. So, this time I suspect suicide, again. See, suicide again.

MASON

Aunt Muffin is not dead, not naturally and not by double suicide. She is aliive and as muffiny as only she can be. She nearly killed me and Kim during the seeming decades that she spent with us. No, Muffin is doing fine.

DAMON

That's it ? You called to let me know that Aunt Muffin came to visit you and Kim. Did her highness spend any of her old money on something new for you or your better half ? No, I suppose not. If she had, you 'd have led off this conversation bragging about whatevever the gift was.

MASON

No, Muffin dispensed no baubles or trinkets to the working class relatives. She left us undazzled.

DAMON

Since when did you become working class ? If you truly were working class, you would be bored like me, and you would join your Kentucky cousin in the daily routine of patrolling the aisles of Krogers, oh excuse me, Harris Tweeters there in Charleston. The grocery store is my sole, brief relief from this awful confinement.

MASON

You may be walking those aisles more than you have been up to now. Aunt Muffin is on her way.

DAMON

On her way where ?

MASON

She is traveling the highway to the wonderful Bluegrass state, to Louisville I say, to be precise. To your not so humble abode, I say to be cruel. She intends to remain with you for a time indefinite in her eyes, and interminable in yours, and unmentionable over a speaker phone in the eyes of your ever lovely wife.

You are her wonderful nephew Damon, the one and only true Button, except possibly for cousin George in Pennsylvania. Damon, the one and only true Button. I'd have that mounted over my mantle if I thought that it would open her purse strings, but she would term such a motivational plaque an extravagance, thereby proving that I merit none of her largess.

DAMON

Are you certain ?

MASON

About you being the one and only true Button ? No, I'm certain that is bull crap. But about her impending landfall at your front door, yes. Hurricane Muffin has a delicious ring to it, although I find Tropical Depression Muffin more apt as a moniker.

Unless she changed her mind in the interim, she told me that she was driving straight through to visit you.

DAMON

When ? Today ? She left your house today ?

MASON

Oh no, not today. It was the day before yesterday, or the day before that. The days just kind of blur into bliss in her absence.

DAMON

Why did you wait to call me until today, Mason ?

MASON

Does it matter ? You have time. As I recall, there is no cooling off period to purchase a handgun in Kentucky. You will be fine.

DAMON

That is not why I asked. You should have informed me sooner.

MASON

I was simply following her majesty's decree. She wanted her arrival to be a surprise.

DAMON

I hate surprises, particulary those involving rich Aunt Muffin And I am already depressed.

MASON

Who isn't depressed these days ?

DAMON

You need another plaque, Mason Button, the sole ecstastic human on Earth. Muffin and virus free.

MASON

I'll get started and carving that later today. But you know, I do feel for the little people.

DAMON

Like me ?

MASON

As far as Muffin is concerned, she may have feared that you would try to escape. I know you Damon, fleeing is in your nature. But you have nowhere to run to.
Her brother refused to let her stay with him, or so I gathered.. I can't stand her when she is healthy.

DAMON

She's sick ?

MASON

She was never healthy.

DAMON

Aunt Muffin has always been healthy.

MASON

Not for me. Now, with this pandemic, she is twice as contagious.

DAMON

I don't want to come down with corona.

MASON

I don't know, Damon. I only mean that she is annoying in normal times. She has so much more to complain about now. Keeping up with her constant barrages was a constant trial. For me as well as Kim, who doesn't need any more stress.

Muffin, arrived, she paused, and now she is gone. I've been spared, that is how I feel plain and simple. I'm free again, if you ignore the planetary restrictions.. Good luck with her.

Do you see now why she didn ;t give you any advance warning ? Sorry, Damon, but I can't regret my complicity. Giving you up reduced my sentence.

Maybe Muffin speculated that you might even consider, now what did you call it, double suicide to avoid the magnificence of her company. Well, I've delivered my message, dear cousin. I must go. Enjoy.

DAMON

Go ? Go where ?

MASON

Where else ? Harris Tweeter. (*call ends and Amy enters, heels clacking*)

AMY

Who was that on the phone, dear?

DAMON

Cousin Mason in Charleston.

AMY

How are things with he and Kim ? It must be better than here, given that they have the beach home and the ocean. But they probably can't even walk the beach now.

DAMON

They may walk in late and night or early mornings. They can't lock out the ocean.

AMY

Why did he call ? He usually just phones to gloat over something or other. Is Kim ok ? She is nice, too nice for Mason. He is such a gloater. Gloat, gloat, gloat. Its disgusting. Its natural that he is proud of what he has accomplished, but..
Kim is ok ?

DAMON

Yes, Kim is wonderful. They are both fine. Aunt Muffin has been lodging with them.

AMY

Ha ! It serves him right. Finally proof of God's vengenance. I'd like to hear Mason gloat now. Gloat, gloat, gloat. Choke on it Mason.
I feel bad for Kim. But she chose him, marry the man, marry the family. I love that expression. Its a shame that Kim will have to live with Muffin and Mason. I pity her.

DAMON

So its Kim duty to put up with Muffin ?

AMY

In so many words, yes.

DAMON

I'm happy to hear you put it in those terms.

AMY

He needs to be taken down a peg, and Muffin is the perfect pin
to his balloon. She will put the end to his bragging.

DAMON

Muffin has left Mason's beach home..

AMY

Oh ? I see now. Muffin departed, but not dearly so. I'm sorry
hon for being snarky. But no one likes your Aunt Muffin, except
possibly herself. I wonder if she has ever looked in a mirror and
told herself, « I like you ».

DAMON

I don't know anyone who does that sort of thing.

AMY

The scourge is gone, and now Mason has called to brag that he
survived a bad case of Muffinitis.

DAMON

I have to agree with you hon. That is exactly what he was
doing, bragging. I should recognize his methods after all these
years.

But there was more news from South Carolina. When you marry the man, you marry the family, right ?

Aunt Muffin is coming to visit us.

AMY

When ?   (*door bell rings*)

Oh no ! No, no, no. I can hear Mason laughing in his crude, gloatful snort. Mason is the worst, a gloater and a snorter. They are a rare breed, regrrettably one not on the promising edge of extintion. What Kim ever saw in that snorting gloater, I will never understand. No, no, no. Muffin is not staying here. We are in lockdown. Where is my mask ?

We don't have an ocean here, why did she choose us ? There is no beach in Louisville.

The angel of death might be on our doorstep this very moment. I don't deserve this.

DAMON

I can assure you honey, Muffin is no angel.

AMY

That woman is bringing who knows what from who knows where. She is covered with it, and if you let her enter, it will be under our roof.

DAMON

It ? Corona ?

AMY

Yes, I T, frigging it, Corona.

DAMON

She just spent a week or so I guess, strange, Mason didn't exactly say how long a time it was that she vacationed in their beach house.

AMY

Vacation ? Muffin wasn't on vacation. The whole planet has canceled their vacation, and now all of a sudden the Button nephews are opening a chain of bed and breakfasts around the country for the benefit of the only surviving vacationer.
Is Muffin an endangered species ? I don't care if she is, that is her choice. But what about us, here in the Kentucky version of Air BNB, or is it hotel california ?

DAMON

Don't overrract.

AMY

« Don't overreact », now playing on MALE radio. Men proclaim «:Don't Overreact » when they have no clue what to do. You don't panic, I'll give you men that.

DAMON

Thanks

AMY

Instead, men freeze up. Men dither. (*doorbell rings*)

DAMON

Muffin is here, just outside.

AMY

She can stay outside until God awakens and strikes her dead. I'll gladly pay the cleanup charges. How did she get to our house. She didn't fly her directly on her broom..

DAMON

Angels don't use brooms..

AMY

She must have stopped at one or more hotels along the journey.

DAMON

Amy, Muffin is family.

AMY

As I am. The difference is that Muffin is rich family.

DAMON

Family is family. (*doorbell rings again, Damon steps to answer the door*)

AMY

And money is money in the best of families.

(*Muffin enters, dressed in expensive but casual clothes, flat shoes, trailing a bag and carrying a very large purse*)

MUFFIN

Good morning Damon. Hello Amy. I was certain that you'd be home, I can't imagine you being an essential worker.

DAMON

I work from my office home all of the time, Aunt Muffin.

MUFFIN

Business casual is certainly not what it used to be. What a slob you've become. Please, at least wear matching clothes. Didn't Mason call and inform you of my arrival ? You're more sloveny than your cousin. He has no excuse, nor do you.

Look at Amy, she's holding up. Your wife has nowhere to go, but she is dressed to go there at the drop of a pin. Bravo, Amy, bravo. That is what we need.

DAMON

I'm Amy's trophy husband.

MUFFIN

Men as trophies? I'll stop laughing next year. At their best they are vacuum cleaners. They excel at some tasks, but overall, they suck.

But, really, the whole country is going to hell. And men like you and your beach bum cousin are leading the way.

Last night, I stopped at a Holiday Inn in North Carolina, or was it Tennesse. Iy doesn't matter which. It was in the

Appalachians. They should do something about those mountains. It has been hundreds of years, and they are still in the way.

Anyway, a man was checking in and asked the receptionist what level of sanitizing they had done beforehand.The clerk was just a clerk, not the head of epidemiology at Johns Hopkins, so she made reference to the chain's normal cleaning routine and their new policy of letting a room set unoccupied for 24 hours between bookings. I ask you, where is the profit in that ?

If you can't travel normally, and accept the rigors of daily life, then don't. People like him should just stay home.

AMY

We should all stay home, Muffin.

MUFFIN

This man, this frightened traveler, was younger than me, I am positive that he was. What a wuss. The restaurants are another disaster. The menus are limited and bland. Amy's cuisine has a real chance now. The three or so restaurants that are still open in this country disperse the customers so far from one another that it is impossible to eavesdrop. What little joy there was in dining alone has evaporated. This virus has put a cap in bad behavior, which is probaly good overall, but has sure ruined my delaying to have dessert and overhearing a juicy confession. No one follows the law.

AMY

Especially you. Why are you even traveling ?

MUFFIN

Someone has to take charge.

AMY

You ?

MUFFIN

Why not ? I have a business to run, an essential business. Two businesses in fact. I will tell you about them sometime.

DAMON

Welcome to Lousville, but I have some bad news.

MUFFIN

I would have arrived here sooner but I stopped at the funeral of an old friend. She was courteous enough to schedule her demise around my travel plans. I'm joking Amy. I am not as callous as many of my family believe. Sometimes, conincidence liberates me from having to live down to my image.

She was a lovely woman. Its a shame that her and her husband's genes were wasted on their children

The funeral was the same as most others, there is only so much that you can do around a dead body. Debutante drama queens approach the casket first, their impatience overwhelms the wisdom of waiting until the perfect moment . They cry and sob, but always have their mascara touchup nearby. None of them wins my awards for showmanship or sincerity.

AMY

I suppose you have no competition in the first category and no hope in the second.

MUFFIN

One of the daughters-in-law had sewn masks for many of the attendees. I say many but there were inexplicable exclusions, she must have understood that this all togetherness that they've been promoting was garbage. She appreciated the immortality of high school cliques. These masks had some football team logo or other. She always did excel at tackiness.

And now of of course, these awful masks at a funeral increase the difficulty of recognizing those that one remeets only in the aftermath of death. One would think that name tags should be mandatory if they are going to require these silly face coverings.

DAMON

Perhaps the daughter-in-law was on the right track, but did not have time to sew on numbers and names.

MUFFIN

I listened attentively to all of words of the service. It was akin to listening to one of those repetitive late night, long commercials that are normally bypassed at warp speed. You know the sort, they play them every seven minutes on FETV.

It was no different than previous sermons. They promised product was, not even a new and improved eternal life. If that was all that they offered, then I'd still pass. Someone, somewhere, must certainly find it attractive, the price seemed reasonable if you craved more of the same existence, but I'm not receptive to that appeal. I couldn't stand more of the same.

And the constant up and down, it was confusing to both heathens and believers alike. By the end of the service, half the attendees had removed their masks in order to catch their breath. Frankly, most of them were more attractive covered.

These sorts of services, they should include a volunteer cheerleader, or have someone preface each rise and fall with « Simon says ».

DAMON

That might add even more confusion, depending on the scripture of the day.

Seriously, Aunt Muffin, I hate to be coldhearted. You cannot stay with us, tonight sure, but tomorrow... We have limited supplies. Basic necessities are nearly unavailable. It is the same for the entire city. You must know that.

Even Derby has been postponed. The colts will be older and stronger by a few months, we may see a new track record set later this year. As I said, common household items are hard to obtain.

AMY

Toilet paper for one.

DAMON

Yes. You can't remain here unless you've brought your own toilet paper. Its basic health and sanitation.

MUFFIN

Well if that is the way you feel. All along the route I was worried about this. Will they refuse my forced invitation ?

I'll stay with someone else. They are greedy enough to welcome me and fearful enough to smile while doing so. I expected you to be different.

AMY

He's not.

MUFFIN

But if you were different Damon, how long would this buy me ? (*Opens rolling bag full of toilet paper*)

DAMON

Two weeks, Aunt Muffin.

MUFFIN

These are worth at least a month. This is the good stuff, vintage Charmin, not the cheap stuff I borrowed from the hotel and the funeral home.

DAMON

Two weeks.

MUFFIN

You are a hard bargainer.

DAMON

It's a fair offer. Its one that goes against my better judgement.

AMY

It goes against me. And common sense. This is all stolen ?

MUFFIN

Theft? Of toilet paper ? Theft is such obscene term for what is more analagous to borrowing, a reallocation of resources. The hotels are large, vacant warehouses full of paper products and cleaning supplies that would be better redeployed to where they are needed. I consider myself a community organizer, a patriot really.

I'm doing this without any thought to payment. The nation can thank me later.

But no, this is not hotel borrowings. I paid for this luxury for myself and a gift to the Kentucky Button family.

Its quality paper, Amy. When was the last time you enjoyed this level of softness ? You should be proud of Damon's toughness.

What if I include this ? (*opens purse and deposits several cans of tuna on a table*)

DAMON

Toss that in, and you can have an additional two days, Muffin.

MUFFIN

This is top of the line, nephew, the best darned canned tuna. You can't find this for love or money. This solid albacore. Well ? (*pause*)

I have another dozen cans in the trunk.

DAMON

All of it is albacore, not that chunk light cheap stuff ?

MUFFIN

Only the best for my favorite nephew and his lovely wife.

DAMON

Alright, you can stay for three weeks.

MUFFIN

What about you Amy ? Are you ok with this ? Look, I
brought this as well. I use it to take my temperature. See, its very,
super high tech (displays quickly and then returns it to her bag). If
this gizmo shows my temperature elevating, I will leave
immediately.

AMY

This is not a good idea.

DAMON

Aunt Muffin, welcome to our house and our neighborhood.
Amy honey, we are not living in a malaria invested jungle.

AMY

Not malaria, but worse.

DAMON

I'll get Muffin settled, it's only for a few days. (*Damon and
Muffin exit*)

AMY

(*Amy agitated while Damon and Muffin are offstage. She
tosses a roll of bath tissue then carefully retrieves it. She stacks
the tuna fish, only to knock the over, then to restack them. Damon
returns.*)

You just sold us into 3 weeks of misery for fish and paper.
She could have easily paid 3000 pieces of silver.

DAMON

Piffle. This is a time for strength, not fear.

AMY

Don't you dare frigging piffle me. You are as deluded as she is. You won't be piffling me as long as she is here.

DAMON

We can't refuse Muffin.

AMY

At the expense of your child's life ?

DAMON

I'm doing this for all our benefit. You know how wealthy she is. Besides, Sawyer is young.

AMY

And that gives Sawyer immunity ?

DAMON

No. I didn't mean that.

AMY

What exactly do you mean ?

DAMON

Our son is young. If something were to happen…

AMY

To us ? You'd expect Muffin to step in take responsiblity ? That word is not in her vocabulary.

DAMON

No, I realize that.

AMY

So ?

DAMON

Well if something happened to the boy..

AMY

His name is Sawyer,

DAMON

We haven't really invested all that much in him. We could have, replacements.
Don't be so judgemental. Look at our sunk costs, they aren ;t that large.

AMY

Please tell me that you are kidding. Your aunt has been here for less than an hour and you are ready to sacrifice everthing for some future inheritance. What about Sawyer's inheritance ?

DAMON

What I'm saying is that Sawyer has nothing to worry about. Nor do we. You saw the thermometer that she has. And she was fine with Mason and Kim.

AMY

Until they sent her packing. I'm amazed that Muffin hasn't tried to kill the virus with the touch and scent of freshly printed money They say that copper works, where are my old pennies ?

DAMON

Well, I'm going down to the man cave, the playoffs are on.

AMY

No, they're not. All sports have been canceled. The only silver lining in this horror.

DAMON

They are rebroadcasting the games from 2012. I forgot who won. (*exits*)

AMY

What are you watching now ?

DAMON

This is the national Cornhole competition. These are the semi finals, live.

AMY

The national Cornhole competition ? If you don't want to answer my question, just say so.

DAMON

I'm serious, Amy. ESPN is reduced to broadcasting cornhole matches. I wonder if the masks are for health reasons or so the contestants may preserve their anonymity, it must be as embarrassing for them as it was painful to watch.

AMY

Then why are you wasting your time staring at the screen.

DAMON

What else am I going to do ?

AMY

If you are willing to just sit and let youself be absorbed by this ridiculous contest, it shows how absurd sports are. Other than the decathlon, competitors derive no health benefit from your their games.

The athletes are like fleshy statues in a sporting mausoleum, paid to wait during extended beer commercials and when play resumes the pace is glacial.

DAMON

Some of the ads are very clever. Its art.

AMY

I have better uses of my time and so do you.

DAMON

What else can I do ? Surf the web ?

AMY

Surfing the web is not exercise, its an excuse to do nothing. You need to get outside more often, and I am not referring to your daily trip to Krogers. You can garden, like me.

DAMON

What have you planted this year? (*loud game noise from the screen*) Oh I missed that. Where is the replay ?

AMY

The usual : tomatoes, green beans, arsenic.

DAMON

Oh, that's nice. You know, this game is not half bad.

AMY

Compared to what ? (*Damon engrossed in game, Amy walks to stand before the mirror*)

I called Kim, but she was of no help. I suspect that if she had any effective Muffin counter measures, then she is keeping them to herself. That is not very charitable of my cousin-in-law, but I'd do the same if the roles were reversed and the dragon was at her gate and not inside
mine. If talk could push Auntie Muffin from my castle, then I'd huff and I'd puff, and blow her out..

(*Muffin, Sawyer, and Kylie arrive home from a walk*)

MUFFIN

I still don't understand the protocol. Is it masks on or off after a stroll around the neighborhood. Is a stroll exercise, or appropriate anti-social distancing ?

Were you talking to the mirror, Amy ?

AMY

No. Of course not. I'm thinking out loud.

MUFFIN

I'd have sworn that you were in deep conversation with the glass.

AMY

I'll leave the deep conversations to you.

MUFFIN

Thinking aloud is the same as chewing with your mouth open.

KYLIE

Muffin is getting to know half the residents in the subdivision. She has introduced herself to more neighbors than I have seen before. She's very friendly.

SAWYER

She stops and speaks to everyone , especially with men. Even strangers.

AMY

Your aunt is a friendly person. She's rarely met a man who hasn't got to know her.

SAWYER

We did more stopping and talking than actual walking. I don't mind though, its great to be out of the house.

AMY

Did you hear that Damon ? A new sport has just been formed in Louisville. You can see it live, tickets are free. And it has the same tortoise like speed that men relish.

KYLIE

We chatted a bit with the widower on the corner. Sawyer and I are in a role reversal with Muffin where we function as her chaperones, otherwise she would stop and chatter with any unaccompanied male.

SAWYER

She does it anyway. I guess that we are failures as chaperones. The widower calls himself Mister Ring. That is such a cool name, I wonder if it is real. Who knows Aunt Muffin, he might be Mister right.

KYLIE

Mister Ring is taking French lessons at the Alliance Française of Louisville via zoom.

SAWYER

Dad, we could do that, too.

MUFFIN

That is a wonderful idea, Sawyer. The Button reunion is next year, and you should know your ancestors' language. Its as important to look backwards as it is forward.

SAWYER

We studied French a few years ago together, remember ? Now that we have all of this free time, can we start again ?

DAMON

That's an idea. I'll look into signing us up. Who else did you chat with, Kylie ?

KYLIE

The man on the next block. 620 is the address. We met so many people today that I forget many of their names.

AMY

Are you encouraging Kylie to speak to odd men ? Or is she bait ?

MUFFIN

Odd men ? These are your neighbors, Amy, not mine.

KYLIE

I thought he would be scary for some reason, but Muffin
started chattering away and he is a very nice man.

AMY

The one who is constantly having home remodeling done ?
He is obsessed with it. The new pool, the new pool redone, the
new garage, the new driveway. It just goes on and on.

MUFFIN

Yes, him, Ernesto. He is proof that life goes on during the
pandemic. He is planning for the future, and hiring workers today.
He is a credit to the community. We have a lot in common.

AMY

He has more more money than sense.

MUFFIN

Excellent qualities in a husband.

AMY

You do have a lot in common, except he spends his money.
The home improvements proove that he can open his walllet.
Plus, Ernesto is married.

MUFFIN

Oh, I've found that remodeling has been known to include a new spouse. Fresh wife, happy life. (*pause*) Don't give me that look. What I said is a life lesson for the children.

AMY

Besides being too married for you, he is too old for you

DAMON

Are you referring to the Spaniard ?

AMY

Ernesto is not Spanish. He is from Argentina.

SAWYER

Yeah, he has three daughters, too. But they are too young.

KYLIE

Too you for what, Sawyer ? They aren';t that young.

DAMON

The Spaniard, excuse me, the Argentenian is only about 50, tops.

AMY

Much too old for you, Muffin. Kylie. Fifty is over the hill for a man. Another life lesson, children, provided free of charge here in the Button residence.

KYLIE

How did you enjoy Charleston, Muffin ? Tell me about it.

MUFFIN

I say Charleston, but Mason's home is simply a beach house
on the Isle of Palms. It has none of the excitement of the city
itself, just the same beach and ocean every day. It was
monotonous. Even the pilgrims left Plymouth rock for some nice
suburbs. Who in their right mind wants to live at the shore ? As
far as Charleston, it was closed. The theaters, and boutiques, all
shut. Ergo, Charleston was closed.

SAWYER

Everything shut down. How long will this last ? A few more
weeks is what they say.

DAMON

This shutdown may be with us for a while longer. It could be
the end of June until the country is back to normal They claim that
the summer heat will end it, but I have my doubts.

MUFFIN

All will reopen. Theaters will reopen. Life is theater, theater
is life. You can't suppress either indefinitely.

AMY

But when ?

MUFFIN

We will laugh and joke about this one day. Not me, perhaps.
Amy, If you are lucky, and I am more unfortunate than I've been

these past years then you will play me and a talent will act you in a sold out Broadway performance.

AMY

Broadway is closed as well.

MUFFIN

Such are the pranks of Life. In the interim, while we await the reraising of the curtain, I'll pretend that theater is dark for a handful of additional nights. I'll ignore bad news and content myself with other art.

I remember the drive through bars of Texas and Louisiana as shining examples of a civilization at its most innovative and courageous

DAMON

Who in their right mind doesn't ? The end of drive through bars was a loss to humanity. What isn't curfewed is closed.

MUFFIN

I pity these governors, no one enjoys being a party pooper, with the possible exception of my late husband. I discovered that during our honeymoon.

If I'm going to expose myself to fiction at this point in my life, it must be art, where the actors are talented and the scripts are entertaining and believable.

AMY

They have closed Broadway.

MUFFIN

As you say.

DAMON

And London, and our own Actors' Theater, and Derby Dinner, and Shelby County, and Little Colonel, and Bunbury.

MUFFIN

The list of casualties is long, that is obvious. Your recitial of the fallen brings joy to no one. Lets talk of art.

You should write art, Damon. There is another writer in the subdivision, we are going for a walk together tomorrow.

AMY

I'd advise him to run.

MUFFIN

We Buttons are born artists, genii with Bohemenian sensibilities.

AMY

A few like you with Rothschild dollars and no sense.

MUFFIN

Art deserves to be rewarded, Amy.

Wealth permitted me to buy a luxurious eccentricity. There are eccentricties and then there are eccentricities. Believe me, all of you.Damon. I paid full price. Eccentricities never go on sale. Contrary to your slight Amy, I've opened my wallet., money flows from in continously, torrents of green like the wake of a cruise ship

I'm old enough to not care, and affluent enough to get away with it.

Damon you are talented, like your uncle George in Pennsylvania. You must speak with him, get his advice on this situation.

AMY

Please return to reality. You talk of art, and escapes, while ignoring the situation as it exists today. I admit having no reasonable guess as to when this will burn itself out. You can't just bury your head in the sand. We are all in this together.

MUFFIN

Only the greedy and the delusional claim that. We are not all in this together. It's another meaningless slogan, designed to control our behavior. That chant had no value in the 1960s and is has not kept pace with inflation since then.
Togetherness won't get you an upgrade to business class.

AMY

No, it won't. Aircraft have become as mythical creatures, slightly more credible than Pegasus. Or do you believe in flying horses ?

MUFFIN

This coming from you ? Each year, you attend the Kentucky Derby Pegasus parade. Who believes in horses on the wing ?

As for togetherness, ask to sit in first class after this silliness is over. You will be all together back in coach, sharing one ration of lifeboat peanuts.

SAWYER

No peanuts Aunt Muffin, allergies.

MUFFIN

Well the heck with that. The airlines can just use the millions of Chinese masks they have been required to waste our money on. These masks, if they can truly protect against viruses, so why not peanuts?

All in this together? Not me. I'm free, I'm traveling, the rest of America can be all together alone, isolated and fearful. I see car tags from every state on the freeways. They are taking their pets with them.
There's an idea. Parents could use pet carriers for children as well as their dogs, using fresh towels for each. Kids harbor all types of germs that are dangerous for animals. As adults, those moments will provide them with pleasant memories. I wonder how large these carriers can be ?

AMY

This virus is real. You seem to believe that this is some mass hallucination. That it is the world of the blind against you, the only human with perfect vision. This is not a play with you as the brave heroine.

DAMON

Amy, remember what you said about your acting back in schoo, how you loved to play the role of villian, and how you wondered why villain was such a pejorative for one so resolute.

AMY

I did not audition for the role of evil in this domestic drama.

MUFFIN

The part comes naturally to you.   Please it is not an insult. I intend that as a compliment to your nature.

DAMON

Aunt Muffin, that was harsh. Regardless of how poetically you form the phrase, there is no complimentary way to tell someone that they clean toilets remarkablly well.

MUFFIN

I'm sorry Amy.

AMY

Maybe this is a stage play. We were happy here with a cast of four.

SAWYER

It was boring, Mom. It was like that French play that I read, *No Exit*. Before Aunt Muffin arrived it was boring and repetitive. We needed a new arrival. I'm glad that Aunt Muffin came to visit. It may not be super fun, but it is interesting.

MUFFIN

Damon, you are uncharacteristicly quiet. What do you say ?

DAMON

There is nothing to do and less to say. I'm drinking tonic water with a hint of gin They say that quinine can prevent catching the virus.

MUFFIN

Does it matter if can or can't ? It's like religion or a ball point pen. You select one that seems to work moderately well and stick with it until it doesn't.

DAMON

We are out of gin. So this is tonic and tonic. Actually, I never stocked much gin. It tastes ghastly. Only the Brits were brave enough to judge it fit for human consumption. I had only one bottle of it. And now it is gone.

Gin and tonic, I think that they misspelled it, it should be called gin and toxic. I hope that it's toxic to the virus.

It contains sugar, two liters is equivalent to one quinine tablet, so that is a lot of sugar, which is not good. But it makes for a sweet placebo.

MUFFIN

Speaking of placebos, I have one here in my hand. This is a fake mask, that I bought because of the fake news. Fake news, how redundant.

SAWYER

You wear a fake mask ? Why ? It looks real to me.

MUFFIN

These masks are sold in every grocery and pharmacy. Packests of 15, available for ten dollars Fabrique en Chine, made in China. Does that strike you as NASA level quality control. This mask is hard pressed to stop a dedicated fart, let alone a microscopic virus.

I also have fake essential papers, this national oppression has been quite motivational.

SAWYER

Fake papers? See mom, Aunt Muffin is awesome.

MUFFIN

Fake essential papers, those are even better.

SAWYER

I bet that you bought them online. What else do they sell ?
Fake ID ? I need to browse that site. Just to see.

MUFFIN

No, I did not buy these. No, not at all. That would be
dishonest. I did it the legal way. I made them myself.

KYLIE

Sawyer told me that you were rich, I mean retired. He said that
you don't work.

MUFFIN

I most certainly do work. I'm saving the country, to the best
of my ability. I'm keeping gas stations and hotels afloat. All I ask
is for a token amount of toilet paper in return.

SAWYER

This story is getting better and better. Aunt Muffin stealing
toilet paper from hotels. Dad, you should take notes.

MUFFIN

Let's be clear, I borrowed it from the hotels, it's not theft.
Damon, I'm out there on the road, doing my bit, more than most, I

expect. And I state this with all modesty. Your wife used to work every day, nursing to various hypochondriacs.

AMY

This virus is real (*shouts*)

MUFFIN

Sure it is. But it keeps the other so-called sicklies at home. It's them that I despise. They have no friends and nothing better to do than clog up the medical system. Health care is overrated. Find a friend, stay healthy.

AMY

That has worked so well for you. Find a friend, stay healthy. Quite a slogan.

MUFFIN

Sarcasm is not your color. You shine in fear. Today you are positively glowing.
Lets's be be practical. What have you done to keep the machinery of our economy running smoothly? Other than staying at home, under the bed?

DAMON

Well…

AMY

He bought a new gun. And who knows how many more bullets. How many more bullets do you need, sweetheart ?

MUFFIN

I've taken to carrying mace and a knife and yes, a small pistol to avoid large difficulties. I may be defenseless against corona but not against my healthy brethren. Three stabbed in Reading England is terrorism, eleven shot in Syracuse is a block party.

The city of brotherly love is in contention for murder capital of the country. I prefer to not be the reason for a magnificent tombstone anytime soon. Definitely not in my lifetime.

AMY

I love your unintended witticisms.

MUFFIN

As I appreciate your absence of intended wit. Knowing my nephew, his gun and ammo are made in America.

DAMON

Unlike Amy's wall of Italian shoes.

AMY

If you and your end of the world friends get your wish of a societal breakdown, make sure that you have a classy outfit to match your weapons. You'll be wearing it for a long time. Me, I'll be the well dressed one. You could do worse than to die in Italian leather. . Just remember, don't shoot women in heels.

DAMON

This virus is real and I don't think it will disappear like a sudden thunderstorm. Chaos may be just around the corner.

AMY

In your dreams.

MUFFIN

Chaos may be coming, but I wager on a brighter future, Damon.   You must be eating poorly, Damon.   You are what you eat. That might be your problem.   Jalapeños always gave my late husband dreams.   He couldn't fulfill his carnal dreams either, nephew.   Something is warping your sense of proportion.

KYLIE

Could it be the tonic water ?

MUFFIN

Who knows ?

AMY

Who knows anything anymore ?

MUFFIN

If it makes you happy, Damon, continue on with buying more armaments.

SAWYER

Telll us again about the essential papers, would you make me a set?

MUFFIN

I don't see why not. (*Hands paper to Damon*) See, it is only a letter, nothing fancy like a notary stamp. This is a free country, have another gun. This is not Nazi Germany.

DAMON

One can hope (*Damon returns the letter to Amy*). I'm kidding, Muffin. I half think that you should be locked up for this farce.

MUFFIN

You are perfectly on point.. Half thinking is one of your skills. Some think, some don't think, but you manage to hit the sweet spot in between without fail. I'm sorry, that was rude, and worse, incorrect. You have so much talent, but sometimes.. (*pause*) Are we still a joyous country ? (*pause*) I wonder.

Oh well, back to this document. I can print you a letter today. If your wife hadn't retired to do whatever it is that she does, her job as a nurse would gotten her one.

AMY

Muffin is correct for once, dear. Why don't we get one for me instead, hon? I bet my nursing friends have them. It would be nice to have one as well.

DAMON

Ok, that makes sense.

MUFFIN

Does it?

DAMON

Well, yes in a way, it does. If something goes wrong and the law gets involved

MUFFIN

Amy would take the fall and not you. You are so gallant.

DAMON

It would be more plausible that she was an ex-nurse coming back to assist during this crisis.

MUFFIN

Oh sure, after all this time. Amy, your husband has a 21st century sense of chivalry; women and children are the first to be sacrificed.

AMY

I know that all too well.

MUFFIN

For these essential papers, we'll have to select a job title that meshes with your abilities.

AMY

Vice President of Finance? (*Muffin rolls her eyes*) No, it needs to be believable and a job that lets you travel.

DAMON

What is your title? (*Damon retrieves the letter from Amy's Muffin's hand, and reads*)
Senior Director of food production for Gemeral Mills. Really? You misspelled General Mills. They can't be aware of this fraud.

MUFFIN

It reads Gemeral and not General. It might confuse the casual reader, but that would be their fault and not mine. It fooled you, and you are smarter than the average bear. The police are used to dealing with documents, it's on them if they don't pay attention to detail. Oh, and to be legal, I registered Gemeral Mills as a company with the Kentucky Secretary of State. It cost me 15 dollars.

SAWYER

That's cool. But why Kentucky ? You don't live here.

KYLIE

Yes, why Kentucky ?

MUFFIN

Why not ? I have one for several states. Its like having foreign currency for various countries. It's just easier. Damon, you know a little about current events, you spend enough time on the internet. I wonnder now if I can apply for one of those free government loans that they are proposing.

SAWYER

A loan for fifteen dollars ? Mom told me that you're rich. Is that true ?

MUFFIN

Its not polite to ask those sorts of questions.

SAWYER

But..

MUFFIN

Politeness has a time and place. And you're right to ask the question. This is not the time for politeness. Yes I'm rich. I want to be richer. As far as any government loan, its really a gift, and it would be rude to turn away a gift. Its not only fifteen dollars, that would not please the government which thinks in much bigger numbers. I have other expenses.

KYLIE

What sort of expenses ? This is free money ? Where can I sign up ?

MUFFIN

Clothes, and with a free loan I can pay the employees their salaries.

SAWYER

You have employees ? I could use a work from home job, like dad.

AMY

So could your father.

MUFFIN

Well there is just me for now.

DAMON

How much does this fake job for a nonexistent company pay you now?

MUFFIN

Nothing, but if the government is willing to invest.

DAMON

This money is not an investment.

MUFFIN

It most assuredly is. It's just like Netflix, or Google, or any of those big Silicon Valley companies. They are pay salaries at first, using investors' money.

AMY

How much would I get? This would be in addition to my stimulus right? I don't want the government to cheat me out of my money.

MUFFIN

We will decide on an appropriate role for you. This is fantastic, the company is really expanding. Did I mention that it helps with speeding tickets, I just point to my sample case on the back seat.
If pressed at one of these unjust traffic stops, and I am not one to be pressed, I inform the officer that the samples are organic spinoffs of Japanese seaweed products. So far, no one has requested a taste.

SAWYER

What if you are stopped by an Asian police office ?

MUFFIN

I also offer a Norwegian based variant.

SAWYER

Aunt Muffin, what if the police call your office to verify your papers ?

MUFFIN

There is no way to check as the phone call routes to my home office voicemail. The courthouses are behaving in the same manner, so I'm following their legal precedence and guidance.

Speaking of which, before they closed, the courts emptied the jails of everyone who ranked below axe murderer. The cells are available but they not accepting guests. They won't be issuing a warrant for me anytime soon.
Crime and punishment have been put in quarantine for the forseeable future. You can purchase anything, guns, drugs, anything except a cut and color. The authorities claim that gray hair in women is a symptom of exposure to COVID.

There is little traffic on the freeways, an intermittent buzz instead of the normal constant drone of passing and passed vehicles. It is a mixture of civilians and combattants in this silent so called war. I wondered how important their individual journeys were compared to mine.

SAWYER

Where these people going?

AMY

Its obvious. They too were driving hellbent to impose on their relatives.

DAMON

I suppose you concluded that yours had more significance, if not priority.

MUFFIN

How could I decide otherwise? If I had, I'd still be back with your cousin up to my neck in sand and saltwater.

AMY

What a marvelous image you describe, Muffin.

MUFFIN

Or worse, sheltering in place at home.

AMY

I would settle for that a first runner up.

KYLIE

So this letter is all that Mrs. Button would need ?

MUFFIN

That is correct. That, and a few props with the Gemeral Mills logo.

DAMON

You haven't stolen General Mills logo, have you ?

MUFFIN

Logo, schmogo. I found an image of something that I liked and use that. Its public domain, obscure but legal. I do have a logo, more or less.

AMY

More or less what ?

MUFFIN

It ;s colorful and its pretty. And its mine, 100% mine as I am part of the public domain.

I don't mess with the US patent office, particularly now. That would be a conflict of interes since they are investors, partners you might say.

DAMON

I see. I was going to ask another question but I fear that the answer would only prove beyond doubt that one of us is insane. Come on Sawyer. (Exits)

MUFFIN

Tell me about the mirror. Is it new ?

AMY

Yes, I was lucky to find it and have it installed before all of this horror began.

MUFFIN

It looks old.

AMY

It is old as well, an authentic antique.

MUFFIN

Are you certain that you weren't talking to the mirror?

AMY

I may have been. What if I were? It's just a way to brainstorm. Other people keep a diary, this is no different.

SAWYER

Mom says that the mirror is haunted. She bought it at Joe Ley's before they closed for good.

AMY

She has only been with us a few weeks.

MUFFIN

She ?

AMY

The mirror. I think that it may be haunted.
MUFFIN

Did Joe Ley's claim that ? Did that increase the price ?

MUFFIN

They said nothing of the sort. It is simply a feeling. In the manner that trees absorb air and sunlight, and sand absorbs liquid, this mirror, a blend of sand and wood, I ask myself, does it continue to the hopes and vanities and fears of those who approach? And instead of just reflecting the image of the current observer, does it also transmit back something of the previous gazers ?

MUFFIN

Are you dipping into Damons' tonic water ? Me, I shine brightly enough, I have no need of added reflection, either my own or that of some captured ghost.

AMY

They say that vampires don't cast themselves in a mirror. Come, stand before this one and let's put it to the test.

MUFFIN

You're silly.

AMY

Indulge me.

MUFFIN

We just came from outside, where the sun is full in the sky. Sunlight kills vampires if not this virus.

AMY

Oh, then you have nothing to worry about

(*Muffin steps to stand beside Amy before the glass, Muffin's arm around Amy before she can move away Muffin smiling and Amy not as she squirms to avoid contact*)

See, there we are, the happy niece and aunt. Neither one of us a bloodsucker. Any more tests?

AMY

Haven't you heard of social distancing ?

MUFFIN

It sounds like a disease, not a cure.

KYLIE

Social distancing is a preventative measure.

MUFFIN

Like a chaperone ?

KYLIE

Yes, like a chaperone .

MUFFIN

I'm afraid chaperones aren't one hundred percent successful either

Does haunted merit a premium or a discount? (*not waiting for a response*) No doubt, it depends on the purchaser, but I suppose that if you've already committed yourself to buy the item, you are willing to pay extra for the phantom. Am I right?

AMY

Maybe. But they included free delivery.

MUFFIN

Have either of you seen this glassy boarder? Male of female? Or perhaps a 21st century ghost with newish sensibilities?

AMY

It is said to be Elizabethan.

MUFFIN

I've been said to be Elizabeathean by some of the younger women in the family.

AMY

I have felt things.

MUFFIN

Well, that is evidence if ever any were needed. (*exits*).

AMY

I wish that Muffin would leave us. Permanently.

KYLIE

We can do that. It would be fun. If it goes well, we might even be able to sell it.

AMY

Sell what?

KYLIE

Why the murder of course.

AMY

What ?

KYLIE

The murder. That is what you mean, murder. Murder in the maison. It might help me get into college, a different university, one far away. When this confinement is behind us, I want to travel, to go somewhere as far away and as different from here as possible. Alaska, South America, somewhere distant.

With the murder, we can sell it online. I'll use the profits to buy a house, or rent a nice one, and retire before I start work. Or just go to school, for enjoyment, and not because I have to study for a career.

AMY

What if we're caught? Murder is still punished severely.

KYLIE

We need to be clever.. I will run the code through thousands of simulations, and some machine learning to be sure. I will have to add some randomizing algorithm to make it addictive.

AMY

What on Earth are you talking about, Kylie ?

KYLIE

Your idea for a new game. I did not realize how up to date you are with the internet. This could be a huge success. another Fortnite. Murder in the Maison, fantastic.

AMY

I am thinking more along the lines of an actual, you know, a rehearsal, so to speak, starting small, a pretended, in a way, not a game per se, not right away, but maybe we could select a test subject.

KYLIE

A mockup ? Like a straw man ?

AMY

Or a woman.

KYLIE

That is a good idea. We need to start somewhere. Since Muffin is here, she could stand in as our model victim. I'm going to do some research right now.

AMY

You must not use the internet for any searches,

KYLIE

Why not ? Don't use the internet ? That is impossible.

AMY

You read every day that the big companies are collecting and analyzing the internet, searching for ideas like ours that they can steal and bring to market in no time.

KYLIE

Yeah, you are right. You have thought this through already, you are just full of great suggestions.

AMY

I've seen enough crime shows to know that the browser history is the first thing that the authorities subpoena. We have to be better, we can't sell a game if we are detected on day one like some neophyte. That won't get you a beach home in Tierra del Feugo.

KYLIE

You're correct again, but I'm not sure that I'd want a beach house in Tierra del Feugo.

AMY

You can research that all you want after our first murder.

KYLIE

To the death of Muffin. (*they bump elbows*)

AMY

This has to be a small team, a team of two. We cannot involve anyone else

KYLIE

Not even Sawyer?

AMY

Especially not even Sawyer. He has teenager scruples. Those are the worst kind. They are erratic, indecphirable, disposable, irrefutable.

KYLIE

Ok. If you say so. But we won't use any of those big words in our game, Amy. Trust me.

AMY

Sorry.

KYLIE

Sorry Sawyer, but no yacht for you. So, getting back to the murder.

AMY

Lets refer to it as the project

KYLIE

Where do we obtain advice if we can't use the web? We can't ask anyone else at all ? This will be impossible. Worse, it won 't be fun. There goes my future. Goodbye beach house. Can we send each other texts or photos ?

AMY

No. Kylie, you live two houses away. No, nothing like that. No electronics. You can do overnights if that would help. We still have an empty guest bedroom.

KYLIE

What kind of game is this? We won't get any likes if we keep this a secret.

AMY

I suppose not. But this is not a game, Kylie.

KYLIE

I understand. It's a school project, a co-op, an experiment.

AMY

Yes, in a way that is what it is, an experiment.

KYLIE

I intend on majoring in finance, not in some CSI curriculum. Can you imagine, working with blood and who knows what? Where is the glamour in doing that, and the hours. Working nights? And have seen where they work, you must have if you've seen any TV shows about it. It's better to just play it as a game. This virus has made that abundantly clear. Not that I wanted to be involved in criminal science.

You'd think that it would be cheaper and equally effective to have criminals sort each other's crimes.

AMY

You have a point.

KYLIE

Like they do in sports.

AMY

They do ?

KYLIE

Absolutely. The teams play one another and determine who wins the championship without any real involvement on the part of the fans. Mostly, they just yell and scream and spend lots of money, with no result on which team eventually triumphs.

AMY

I see. Now, about our rehearsal.

KYLIE

Yeah, sorry. I sometimes get distracted.

AMY

Kyle we all get distraction. I have had a big one for a week now.

KYLIE

If Muffin, as our test subject number one. I'll just refer to subject one going forward. If subject one were to die of anything, we could make it look like COVID.

AMY

The authorities would check.

KYLIE

Yeah. So ?

AMY

They would determine that it wasn't COVID

KYLIE

Yeah. So ?

AMY

Whoever investigates would tell the truth.

KYLIE

Not in my game. It will be modeled on real life, where not everyone tells the truth. It's more rare than you think, Amy. Especially when it comes to telling the truth about important things.

AMY

Why won't the investigator tell the truth? (*Amy perplexed*)

KYLIE

Yesterday, you referred to Sawyer and myself as children. I'm not a kid, Amy. If I were, I wouldn't call you Amy. I understand how the world works and how it doesn't work.
Hospitals and the media want every death to be caused by COVID.

AMY

This damn virus doesn't merit a one word name like Elvis.

KYLIE

We will oblige them. This is hilarious. Imagine, Amy, the state powers will be our will accomplice. Like Muffin and her government investors. She has weird ideas too, but I agree with many of them.

The police won't investigate on their own as they are as frightened as most people.

AMY

Aren't you ?

KYLIE

No. You are. I can see it in your eyes. Your wearing the mask so often here, in your own home, is proof. I'm surprised that you don't have it on now.

AMY

When you aren't here..

KYLIE

Sawyer infroms me that you sometimes wear it when you are alone with just him. Or is it Muffin, that you fear? It doesn't matter. Fear of this virus is just so widespread.

This murder would make a great movie, who could play me ?

AMY

We can't tell another soul.

KYLIE

The movie will have to wait until after the video game. I heard that all film production has been suspended.

For the murder, Muffin, sorry, Subject One, could stumble and fall, striking her head on a convienetly places hard object, and Monsieur Covid would be Suspect One.

Do you remember the case of that homicide detective who was shot and murdered a year ago in Cave Hill cemetery?

AMY

I do. Detective Percheron. He lived in the subdivision. But you know that. What about him?

KYLIE

If the murder had happened this Spring, his death would be attributed to COVID, although as far as I know, the virus doesn't own a gun.

AMY

In the case of our own Subject One, what would be the true cause of death? Surely not some hard to arrange tumble down a staircase?

KYLIE

Poison?

AMY

D o you know much about poisons? I don't. (*Kylie shakes her head*). A car accident?

KYLIE

That is almost as difficult to do correctly as a staircase slip, but is more certain. Plus if you don't succeed at first, you don't have to schlep the subject back up the flight of stairs. You just back up and zoom over her again. Teenage boys would like that scene a lot.

AMY

Who? Which teenage boy?

KYLIE

The gamers, they like to boom, zoom, smash. Boys, but husbands too. Do you think that it is true what they say about boys and men.

AMY

Yes, I guess so.

KYLIE

Its's funny. With our game, the price of their toy would be the same for both.

AMY

Possibly for the game, a car would be ok. Like you said, for the boys. But there must be girl gamers, you, for example. Me, I'd regret damaging my car. And to back up and zoom, maybe a few times to be sure, zoom, zoom. No, not yet. One more zoom for good measure.

KYLIE

We can use her car, not yours. She won't need it afterwards, regardless of how many zooms are on the vehicle.

AMY

Except the vehicle would pass to me, to us, to Damon and me. And Sawyer will need a car when he goes away to college, whenever that is. I just hate thinking about him driving a car chock full of zooms, it can't be good luck to be zooming back and forth to school in a car with such a history.

KYLIE

You are taking this game far too seriously, Amy.

AMY

You are also. I'm glad that we are. As you said, we need to be clever. This is a question of money versus design.

KYLIE

It is ? (*pause*) How about a gunshot ?

AMY

I had the walls painted before the holidays.

KYLIE

Are you and Ernesto down the street in some sort of competition ?

AMY

That's nonsense. It was painting, not a seventy thousand dollar swimming pool
I dont't want to suffer that disruption again. Besides, the painters aren't available. If they were I would not want them in my house. Their presence would only compound the problem that I need to resolve.

KYLIE

Alright, no falls, no car accidents, no gunshots. If only you knew a doctor who could fake a death certificate. Documentation is key, its essential.

AMY

Essential documentation (*aloud but to herself*). Gemeral Mills, experimental food samples, poisoned accidently by Muffin herself. Poisoned Muffins, I like it.

KYLIE

What do you like ?

AMY

A solution, Kylie. We can discuss this more tomorrow.

KYLIE

Sure Amy. I will see you tomorrow. (*exits*)

AMY

(aloud to her reflection)
Now to purchase one of those burner phones at Krogers. The internet makes for a wonderful accomplice as long as we remain anonymous plotters. I feel better than I have since her arrival, knowing that soon she will be among the departed. I can order an

outfit funeral from Prime, yet that would dress me in premeditation. The celebration will need to wait. Really, its self defense. I'm at hero at work.

KYLIE

(*Kylie enters wearing a mask*)
Hi Amy. I was going to text, but you said not to, so I came over instead. I'm not feeling great today, it may just be that time, but, it pays to be careful. I might have a slight fever, that's the reason for the mask. Do you have a thermometer that I might use. I can wait outside.

AMY

No, just remain there by the door. I have a thermometer upstairs. (*Turns to mount the stairs*)

No, wait a minute. Muffin has one of those high tech marvels in her bag. She isn't here to ask permission.

KYLIE

She enjoys trolling for men at ths time of day. Are you sure that looking in her bag is ok ?

AMY

I'm positive. Medical emergencies take priority.

KYLIE

Alright, since you say so.

She has the biggest purse of anyone. These are just papers, bank statements, brokerage statements, another bank statement.

AMY

Maybe I should take a look at those, but no, I can't. That's not appropriate.

KYLIE

It is her private information.

AMY

I meant because you might be sick. I can't look. But you can.
Muffin is family after all.

KYLIE

Wow. She is incredibly wealthy. Sawyer said rich, but he has
no idea. If I didn't have a fever before, then these numbers would
have elevated my temperature just as much.

So far no thermometer, just this small pistol.

AMY

Be careful with the gun.

KYLIE

Don't worry, I'm American.

AMY

And what is this ?

AMY

Have you found it the thermometer ? It looks like a ray gun or
a water pistol.

KYLIE

(*pulls device from bag*) This ?

AMY

Yes, that is the thermometer. Muffin showed it to us on her first day.

KYLIE

Are you sure

AMY

Yes, I'm sure. I only saw it the one time, but the thermometer is quite disctinctive.

KYLIE

This is not not a thermometer, Amy. It is just a water pistol with a number, 98, glued on to the back.

AMY

(*collapses onto a chair*)
What ? That can't be right. All this time…

KYLIE

(*sprays water pistol with sanitizer by the door so that Amy can approach and inspect it*)
Come, see for yourself. This is just a toy.

AMY

Nothing but a toy. How could she ? The better question is, how couldn't she, its her nature. Playing games in the middle of a war. I could just crush this (*goes to stomp the toy but decides not to*)
Muffin is putting us all at risk. She flirts with every stray man in the subdivision. I can imagine what she carries into the house with her. My house.

KYLIE

Amy ? (*Amy regards Kylie*) Muffin wears what she calls a fake mask. She carries a fake thermometer, she flaunts fake essentiel papers. Are these statements just as false ?

AMY

No, they are real. Her mail is arriving here now, and I recognize some of those envelopes. Muffin never jokes about money.

Kylie, please put everthing back as you found it. I have an oral thermometer in the upstairs medicine cabinet, you know where it is. Run upstairs and check your temperature. I'm so boiling mad that the thermometer would likely explode in my hand. I need to think for a few minutes.

(*Kylie rearranging items during Amy's talk, then exits*)

(*Amy before mirror, holding papers and toy that she has removed from Mufifin's purse*)
She told us « Other rich people are secluding themselves in exclusive private estates rented at astronomical rates, I content myself by cozying up with you and Damon »

Until now, cozy had a pleasant connotation. Its now a vulgar four letter word

We can have Muffin or her money. It's an easy choice, mercenary on one hand and defensive on that same hand. She can pay and stay or leave and live.

Living here is not free of charge. And yet it is the same for we as she. What good is money once dead. No, it is fine if she leaves and removes a threat from our home, more profitable if she slides horizontally from this abode.

These papers promise us a better life once hers is ended, while this garish placebo assures dear Muffin of a cozy sejour among us. She mocks and threatens our very existence.

She must die.
My utmost efforts to force her out have failed. Damon does his best to be a man, he dithers.
Muffin must die.
There, I've said it. And her death must be more than an electronic version. She must die for real if I am to live for real.
I wont dither but ponder.
I will grant her a few more days, while my plot remains in incubation

(*Amy returns items to bag*)

(*Kylie returns*)

KYLIE

All is well.

AMY

Or soon will be.

KYLIE

What did you say ?

AMY

How is your temperature?

KYLIE

Normal. I'm fine.

AMY

Good. Great. Me too. I hope that you are as energized as I am. Since you are feeling well, let's review where you are with the project, perhaps we are ready for a story board dry run.

I have thought ahead about merchandising. We could have our own clothing line for the murder game. It's never too early to plan for expansions and spinoffs. And I thought that I might order a new black dress for our rehearsal. But I really hate to tip our hand by searching online.

KYLIE

I don't see where buying a black dress would raise suspicions.

AMY

No, maybe not. What I need is for someone I know to die before subject one, not someone too close to me, that would be sad for me. But not a total stranger either.

KYLIE

Why not a total stranger. What could be easier? Just read a real paper, they still print those I think, and select the obituary of a real or plausible acquaintance. Use the internet tracking to your benefit. Then order a black dress for overnight delivery.

AMY

I might order several and return all but one.

KYLIE

Lots of us order in multiples. It's less suspicious now that you mention it.

AMY

I'll expense it as a game development cost.

DAMON

(*In a Zoom meeting, during which he can don headphones, and prowl the room, using any props as desired*)

Hi Doris. How are things in your cabin ? You are the envy of half the country. Our Kentucky lockup has a new prisoner, my Aunt Muffin. She is quite a handful.

DORIS

The Button gang has finally been bottled up ! The world can rest in peace. I thought that Muffin was very pleasant, not like my stepmother. She lived down to the term. I used to have to milk the cows each morning before walking two miles to school.

DAMON

Celebrities would pay good money for that sort of rehab. They need their decompression time. As far as the rest of the world, yeah they can rest, but my life is more stressful. I'm in a race that I can't win. Neither can any of the other contestants, that is writers and artists. The opening gun of this pandemic race was not a starter pistol but the sound of an executioner's weapon, we were already consigned to artistic death, it was just a matter of time. We heard the shot before the bullet's impact.

DORIS

Well sheet Damon. I thought that you might be depressed before I called. I could not have been more mistaken. You aren't letting this situation get you down one tiny bit. But you are dressing slovenly. Don't you do laundry ? Look at me.

DAMON

You remain a sharp dresser, Doris. Are the earrings new ?

DORIS

As a matter of fact they are, I made them myself. With a little help from Buddy.

DAMON

Which Buddy ?

DORIS

Buddy, my Spitz. We go on walks together, he even helps me garden. That is how I got these earrings. Spitz dug them up.

DAMON

He did ?

DORIS

Not the finished product, Damon. That would be incredible.

DAMON

Yeah, I don't know what I was thinking.

DORIS

No, for something like that, you'd need a different sort of dog. Definitely not a Spitz. A golden retriever would be the obvious candidate. Buddy found the stones, I polished and mounted them. Good old North Carolina jewels are more than good enough for me. (*pause*) . How is Amy doing ?

DAMON

Better than me, now that I think about it. Like everyone else is doing better than me. But especially Amy. She seems chipper these past few days.

DORIS

I
Good for her. I bet she dresses well, too. Damon, you pretend
to have a tough life now with the virus, its fantasy, and I am not
buying that crap. I should send you one of my uphostery needles so
that you can prick and burst your private pity bubble.

DAMON

I'm not that bad. You should write a self help book.

DORIS

I have talent to sew thread in these fingers, but you still have
the the ability to sow stories with yours. Do you want to hear what
I do to remain sane?

DAMON

Remain sane ? I doubt that you and sanity inhabit the same zip
code. Are you sure that it is working for you?

DORIS

That is the spirit. It may not be as effective as I choose to
believe it to be. but, listen, this is free advice. I talk to my
reflection. You know, mirror, mirror on the wall, who's the fairest
and all that.

DAMON

Not you as well ? Is this a new old fad among women your
age ?

DORIS

My age ? Hey, I'm still your boss, or at least your editor. Do I
detect gender and age insensitivity ? If so, good, that is what you
are paid to write. This mirror thing, I'm serious. It sure as hell
beats posting on Facebook, where seldom is heard a non
disparaging word. Try it sometime. But not now. I want to discuss
your work.

DAMON

There is a bartender here at a local place.

DORIS

Is this a joke ?. I said that I want to discuss your work.

DAMON

This is work.

DORIS

What about him?

DAMON

It's a she.

DORIS

Uh huh. Reflect well before you utter another word. I've
known you and Any for a long time. I don't want to hear things
that I'll regret being aware of.

DAMON

Don't jump to conclusion. This young woman.

DORIS

They are always young women.

DAMON

Please, let me continue

DORIS

Is she attractive?

DAMON

Beauty is in the eyes of the beholder.

DORIS

I take it then, that the majority of the men in this bar are beholding her ?

DAMON

She has numerous tattoos. They tell her life story, the story that she elects to tell.

DORIS

This reminds me of a very old story, Damon. Do you believe her tale ?

DAMON

I am ignoring you. Catherine, this young woman, is recounting her story in ink, just as I've been trying to do with marginal success I'm not sure whose writing is more shallow. The fact is that her book is out there, visible, publicized, garnering the attention of readers. While my readers either hibernate or shrivel and disappear.

DORIS

It would be both expensive and painful to inject one of your novels into your body. I cannot envision you standing in public like a literary Times Square cowboy, while passersby raise your arm and spread your cheeks to pass from one chapter to another. You bemoan your absent readers. I'd have deployed a more descriptive word, but hey, you are the writer, not me. What is the true point of this colorful tale, Damon.? Self pity? Jealousy ?

DAMON

I don't know

DORIS

Then forget any point, focus instead on the emotion, capture that passion and turn it into a great story. By the way, is Catherine pretty ?

DAMON

You have a one track mnd.

DORIS

Forgive me Damon. I'm pretending to be a man today. It's so relaxing only having to think about the same one thing all day long. I just put myself on autopilot obsessing about sex, and poof, all of a sudden the day has passed by, I switch back to woman mode. I take a bath and go to sleep. I do this at least once per month.

DAMON

Doris, I've rarely seen you this feisty.

DORIS

Its the fresh North Carolina mountain air. I live at high elevation to compensate for being short. See, we all have our crosses to bear.

Where was I?

DORIS

Dreaming about your barmaid?

DAMON

No. Are you this snide with all of your writers?

DORIS

Only the male ones, it's effective as motivation. Are you writing ?

DAMON

Some. I am stuck in the house and yet I have no solitude.

DORIS

Solitude is fabulous for writing classic works of fiction. The only sales of that crap are to folks who use it for compost. Ashes to ashes and dust to dust for the authors as well as their works.

DAMON

You aren't hesitant to render harsh verdicts.

DORIS

I neglected to mention those who purchase masterpieces by the ton in order to fire their green fireplaces for amusement. Better to ignite the past than to burn the future.

DAMON

I'd like to feel some of that burn.

DORIS

What ?

DAMON

I'd be satisfied if I sold enough books to have them shoveled by the bushel into some future furnace.

DORIS

You are preaching to the proverbial choir. These greens are too lazy and too hesitant to take axe to oak, while the tree is probably dying from some goddamned insect from China. Can't they consider it plant euthanasia? I really want to write an article or even a real book about these folks, but my attorneys forbid it.

DAMON

Have you reviewed my latest book idea ? What say the
lawyers ? More importantly, what say you ?

DORIS

No.

DAMON

Brief and to the point, excellent qualities in a 300 dollars an
hour vacuum.

DORIS

As are our former readers. I am sorry Damon, but no one buys
it, and even fewer read it. We are on the downward slope of
literacy. (*Pause*)
Unless..

DAMON

Hope spoken in two syllables.

DORIS

True crime.

DAMON

Two more utterances of reprieve.

DORIS

If you could write something delightfully deadly, light but
lethal, heart warming yet blood curdling.

DAMON

I can do that.

DORIS

It requires a big man to bow down, but the result can be

DAMON

Awards ?

DORIS

Better than awards, profits. Oh, Damon, your disgust zooms across the internet in color if not in warmth.

DAMON

I am not a complete philistine, damn the samaritain in my family tree, for if I were, I'd have more success with our so-called readers. Once I learned to read, I thought myself talented enough to write. Wrong again. Life may be a joke, but in it I have my own solemn skit to perform.

DORIS

What about this true crime?

DAMON

Are you serious?

DORIS

True crime (*said in a deep tv voiceover manner*)

DAMON

Is our zoom being hacked ?

DORIS

Yeah, we're likely being hacked. The entire world is hacked. I wish I was a hacker.

DAMON

Instead of being a hack?

DORIS

Listen Damon.

DAMON

I have little else to do except to listen.

DORIS

Killing a hacker is a public duty, like wearing a mask. A new normal.

DAMON

I despise that expression as much as you hate hackers.

DORIS

So kill one.

DAMON

I don't know any, killing him or her would prove difficult.

DORIS

Creativity is your gift. Create a hacker, track him down and kill him. In about 60 thousand words, fewer if you have photos.

DAMON

Where do I find photos of this phantom hacker ?

DORIS

That is a naive question. Where have you been for the past few decades? Make up the story, make up the hacker, make up the photos if you're tired of writing sixty thousand unread words. Just kill somebody. And don't make the victim some 99 year old widow in a nursing home in Seattle.

DAMON

Yes, I heard. I was sorry to hear about your mother. She was a good woman.

DORIS

See, you can be creative ! You never met my mother. Damon, please, just kill someone. If you have to do some research..

DAMON

What sort of research?

DORIS

How would I know ? Writers are always doing their damned research. I'm a hack and an editor, I do my own sort of research, you do your own. Whatever gets you in the mood to spill blood. Just expense it. But keep it reasonable. The IRS is less amenable to crime than..

DAMON

Than who ?

DORIS

I don't have the answer to that question either. Maybe the damned hackers. Damon, I tell you this as your editor and friend, just kill someone. We'll talk again soon. Bye. (*exits*)

DAMON

(*Damon approaches and stands before the mirror*)

True crime? Murder? Have I sunk that low? A fake true crime to save my career? A genuine garroting would be more noble to my dark soul and my void bank account's hunger for blackness. She will die anyway.

Are you there, COVID, staring back from your own ebony abyss? What counsel you, or are we competitors ? I prefer collaborators.

I warrant top billing in this affair. Fame is the name I wish to append to mine, whereas you, my microscopic misanthrope, you offer nothing more than dust to your charges. I choose to run the odds, against the hackers, the slackers, against public and my personal evil.

(*Damon toys with various scene props, testing them as weapons, pretending to stab,bash,choke,garrot an imaginary victim*)

Fame never succumbs to oblivion. Yes it is evil versus evil, so I will wager all on the former. All I lack is a victim, the pickings are thinner than slim, but with my dagger (*holding pen like a short Scottish knife*) I will find a suitable victim. (*Laughs theatrically*)

If it is crime that satisfies then nothing is more filling than murder. But murder is mushy, poison is precise

(*Muffin enters*)

DAMON

Good morning, Aunt Muffin. How was your walk ? Or did the fog deter you ?

MUFFIN

I'm not about to walk in this whiteout, not at my age. I like my hips as they are. I couldn't see much beyond my feet in these conditions, and then you have the cyclists.. They must all be working from home, so they gather together like boys on summer breadk. Grown men who dress themselves in their official Tour de France clothing. Goodness, they are more costume than anything else. I hate to say this, but they should take fashion lessons from you, Damon. You dress like the old fart that you are. And then these cyclists slalom down Oakhurst like they are descending the Maritime Alps ouside of Nice. It's pathetic.

DAMON

And dangerous for the aunts of old farts ?

MUFFIN

I tell myself, it could be worse, they could be sheltering in place.

DAMON

Things are different now. I miss the biweekly visits of our housekeeper. It was a semi-monthly for Amy and myself. I thought of her like a doctor, one who visited our home twice a month, and a few hours later, left behind an immaculate and healthy household.

Maybe I could use that as a plot for Doris.

MUFFIN

Doris who ?

DAMON

Is there poetry suspended in this pen, requiring nothing more than the warmth of my hand to make it flow ?

A down on his luck widower homeowner kills someone to acquire the regular services of a skilled cleaner. But the deed would need to be done outside the home, as the widower could not risk that his desired housecleaner become instead the prime witness to his crime. That would be too Greek.

MUFFIN

Are you on some sort of Bluetooth call with this Doris?

DAMON

No, sorry. I was just rambling myself. Doris Tipton is my editor and my periodic kicker in my backside. Before I forget, I want to inform you that the day after tomorrow is Sawyer's birthday.

MUFFIN

Thanks for the reminder. I have gift for him.

DAMON

He is at the age where he no longer appreciates it but Amy is making a cake for him. Not a cake exactly, but she is baking cupcake muffins for everyone, each with their own letter on top.

MUFFIN

That is more clever than I thought Amy possible.

DAMON

Oh she can bake. But they say that with COVID you lose sense of taste. Just the other day,Amy mentioned that her sense of taste has diminished. She claims that her meals lack flavor.

MUFFIN

They always have. What about your senses ? Does Amy still disguise the taste of arsenic on your plate ?

DAMON

That is cruel, even for you.
MUFFIN

I'm waiting for a response. You know what she is like.

DAMON

After two decades of marriage, I'm immune. Or Amy has

MUFFIN

Changed ?

DAMON

Perhaps.

MUFFIN

Change is impossible.

DAMON

Then I wager that she considers another 20 years with me as being preferable to 30 in prison.

MUFFIN

That isn't what I meant by clever.

DAMON

What then ?

MUFFIN

The letters on the cupcakes or muffins, or whatever it is that she is cooking up.

DAMON

What about them ? It's nothing special. Just the first letters of our names.

MUFFIN

Yes, exactly. Muffin, Amy, Sawyer, and Kylie. M A S K.

DAMON

I see now. What a coincidence. But what about me ?

MUFFIN

M A S K D, masked. So what do you have planned for today ?

DAMON

I'm going to the post office.

MUFFIN

Wow. I am impressed.

DAMON

If that impresses you, then this will rock your world. It certainly rocked mine. Guess.

MUFFIN

Are you forming a band ?

DAMON

A band ? No. A band ? At my age ? Although I coud try my hand at writing music.

MUFFIN

What do you know of music ?

DAMON

Absolutely nothing.

MUFFIN

Good, then you have no bias, no misconceptions. So I was correct on my first guess ?   But a song is a three and a half minute race. Writers are the endurance athletes.

DAMON

My editor would disagree. It is not music that she suggested that I turn to.

MUFFIN

Not the media.

DAMON

Well, not the news…

MUFFIN

You remember your great aunt Trudy, in Pennsylvania. She holds a reunion every three years or so. I haven't seen Trudy in a few years. Strange, now a few years is that remain to either of us.

The last time I visited, the large Hemlock tree in her yard had been topped, and subsequently commenced to grow in all directions. It was a slow, speed of wood thrashing, the once magnificent patriarch forced to contort itself into some monstrous bush, like an impoverished millionaire reduced to begging. It was as if the hemlock tree was dying of self poison.

That is the media business.

Damon, you are fortunate to not be a reporter. Stick to writing meaningful articles.

I was so hopeful that the internet would finally put the bed wetting media out of business. Regrettably, it's proven to be nothing more than a great big dierutic, and that pisses me off.

DAMON

Well it would now, wouldn't it?

MUFFIN

Technology is supposed to be for our benefit, it should have dried up the newspapers for good. And then there are the popups on webpages, sub lethal booby traps, that launch in the most obnoxious of ways. They are like a first date, where the other person wants to move in with you simply because you ordered an appetizer. For forty years the media has been advising its viewers not to trust authority, except them of course.

They lost their credibility when they began referring to themselves as journalists instead of reporters. Grade inflation is what it is.

DAMON

So who should one believe?

MUFFIN

Whoever, it doesn't matter, the experts reverse direction as quickly as a running back.

DAMON

As rapidly as a politician?

MUFFIN

That's a whole different level of skill. One invents politicians as easily and as foolishly as one creates gods and demons. We do it with the best of intentions, selfishness is the motivation.

DAMON

They relieve us of responsibility. And worry, I imagine. We can rest easy, pretending that we are safe. We can dream in comfort, more or less. . We can dredge up dream after dream. Lately, have you noticed it, the politicians are becoming pretty.

MUFFIN

I swear, these reporters and politicians are semi grown adults who never received enough attention as children. They understand no other behavior except to whimper, and pout, and tattle. These young reporters carry themselves worse than any of my friends.

DAMON

How many of those exist ?

MUFFIN

Friends?

DAMON

Yes, friends. How many friends do you have ?

MUFFIN

Enough. Don't worry about conducting a census. The old reporters have been replaced a million to one, drama queens who possess no gift of language, and worse yet , they have no concept of an editor, someone who would filter the worst of their idiocy. Free speech is worth its price.

DAMON

Everybody has an opinion. Let me tell you about my editor's. True Crime.

MUFFIN

True Crime ?

DAMON

True Crime.

MUFFIN

I don't understand, Damon. Is True Crime your editor's opinion, or is True Crime your editor's name ?

DAMON

Why her name, I mean her opinion of course.

DAMON

Her opinion is True Crime. Well, she is can certainly edit, but I think in this case she may have gone much too far.

DAMON

On that you and I agree. She has gone too far. However, too far is undoubtedly where I need to end up.

MUFFIN

What is intended by True Crime as an opinion. Is she in favor of it ?

DAMON

Yes. That is what she suggested that I write.

MUFFIN

Oh ! I get it.

DAMON

Imaginary or real, true crime sells.

MUFFIN

Imaginary true crime, I see. I prefer Sartre to the Bard. The Frenchman understand that there is more sorrow than spilled blood in life. But the audience elects who they will, they adore violence and murder. People may no longer read either of the two dead European playwrights but their lust for killing remains unabated.

You should write true crime, then. But I don't proffer advice. You aren't as foolish as your parents, by parents I mean include only your mother, but parents is less sexist. You know, when I was your age sexist was not a word, sextant was of course, as was sex, but both were equally unfamiliar.

Your mother, she married your father without being pregnant. That speaks volumes as to her courage if not her wisdom. You have both.

DAMON

Hold that thought. I will return in a minute. (*exits*)

MUFFIN

I notice the others, too absorbed by this square of glass and wood. I quit Charleston for the sun of Kentucky, but I find that although the days grow longer, this house grows darker by the hour. This dwelling is beyond somber.
It needs comedy, not crime. It demands a shared activity, not a game, an evening without losers, only participants, no competition, only family

(*Damon and Amy enter, She wearing a nice dress, in heels, with an apron and a broad rimmed hat, carrying gardening utensils*)

That is quite the gardening ensemble. Heels ?

AMY

I can dig and aerate simultaneously. Do you care to join me ?

MUFFIN

I remain as far away from dirt as possible. It is a constant reminder of my own upcoming planting. Despite the most careful, expensive, and liturgical gardening efforts, I won't resprout the following spring to live again. My life is but a day, and the sun is past noon.

AMY

Wonderful mushrooms can emerge when the sun is blocked.

MUFFIN

A mushroom patch is a horrid vision : moist earth,in the darkness, lightly rooted to decaying neighbors. But to each her own, Amy.

Gardening. It makes me shiver equally. Kneeling in the damp with a trowel, accidentally slicing worms in half. I just know that the newly formed pair will remember the injury and pay back the insult in double on me at some future rendezvous. My poor knees, they are intended for flexing at the golf tees, not for kneeling among the bees.

DAMON

I do not picture you ever on bended knee, Muffin

AMY

At least not just one knee.

MUFFIN

My joints are still mine, and I will not risk an overpriced operation for the sake of a prize winning geranium.

AMY

Instead of gardening Muffin, have you considered yard work as exercise?v You might dig a hole and refill it.

MUFFIN

Damon, did I hear correctly? Please repeat Amy's suggestion?

AMY

I said, you might dig a hole in the backyard and fill it back in.

MUFFIN

With a trowel? That is for babies at the beach. I saw that a few weeks ago on the Isle of Palms.

AMY

WWe have a full size spade, you could excavate a much larger hole.

MUFFIN

(*Laughs*). My apologies. I realize that you are serious. Thanks for the offer, but no thanks. The process strikes me as a prisoner's punishment. Is that what I've become?

AMY

It's not you the prisoner. (*pause*) It would be good exercise, that's all.

MUFFIN

Digging my own grave? Who would refill it?

AMY

That would be an oversubscribed offering, we'd receive more hands than available handles.

AMY

You have had bizarre ideas previously, me in your garden is a blue ribbon that will remain unawarded. I will stick with my neighborhood walks. Thanks for the suggestion. If you want to dig, go ahead. It probably helps to clear the head of misguided thoughts.

(*Kylie and Sawyer enter*)

DAMON

I noticed the heavy fog earlier Kylie. It kept Muffin inside. Did you venture out ?

KYLIE

I love the fog. It dissolves realtiy into a world vague, unclear, mysterious. It oscillates between warmth and chill. . Fog is nature's mask. It reminds me of a veil.

DAMON

Diaphanous is the word.

KYLIE

I like the sound of that word. Diaphanous. The morning fog wraps itself like a cool, moist kiss over your entire body. People and objects emerge from the mist like characters appear suddenly when you turn to anew page in a book. Familiar becomes unfamiliar and vice versa.

Fog is much better than a rainbow, not as pretty, but better. I can immerse myself in its cloak, I hide inside and I am whatever I want to be. For a while, until the sun intervenes and ruins the moment.

I can't imagine living in a place that never enjoys fog.

MUFFIN

Damon, you have some competition under the roof in the wordsmithing category.

SAWYER

Kylie will make a great Button.

MUFFIN

Oh !   That reminds me. There is a new Button on the way. Kim is expecting.

KYLIE

Kim who ?

DAMON

Mason's wife Kim ?

SAWYER

How long is she going to be pregnant? (*others stare at him*)

MUFFIN

The normal duration, I expect. Unless she is obstinate or impatient. Obstinancy is futile and impatience is suspect.

SAWYER

No, I mean, when is she due ?

MUFFIN

She just found out before I left their Isle of Palms home. That was one reason for my departure.

KYLIE

That was very considerate Muffin.

MUFFIN

Ha. I didn't think so. I had to leave. Pregnant women can be so annoying.

Normally, Kim rattles on incessantly, and now pregnant, the talking would never end. That woman can talk you out of anything, especially her house.

Don't spread a word of this to Mason, especially not you Damon. You like to capture my words and spread them like an arsonist's accelerants immediately before family reunions. We have one bonfire, we don't need any one burned at the stake. Particularly not me. No Kylie, I don't think this pregnancy was very considerate at all. And if Mason learns my true feelings, he would impregnate his trophy wife several more times, just to annoy me.

KYLIE

You have an issue with annoyance.

MUFFIN

Absolutely.. It is one of those items that is better to give than to receive. Mason and Kim are members of the idle class.

AMY

Aren't you a member of the idle class as well ?

MUFFIN

I've earned my situation, Kylie. I worked very hard to get where I am. Some of us have the luxury of time, or the luxury of money.

KYLIE

Or the luxury of indifference ?

MUFFIN

Yes, the first two luxuries can pay off indifference. But, I'm not indifferent, although I pity the saints who over care. They'd be more content, if not happier, if they'd throw up their hands and surrender to being typical human being.

KYLIE

Then they wouldn't be saints. That is my point.

MUFFIN

Mine, too. I've earned my luxury of wealth. On the other hand, the South Carolina beachcombers have too much time free time. You see what happens ? Youth has the excuse of inexperience. Mason is old enough to know better.

AMY

That is absurd. You've earned the right to relax, not the right to mock the decisions with which your disagree. Muffin, you do love to misconstrue what is said and in this case, Kim's pregnancy.

MUFFIN

I only misconstrue what you say, Amy. Others, I construe well.

AMY

I have no doubt. And twice on Saturday nights.

SAWYER

Was the pregnancy planned ?

MUFFIN

Without any question it was planned. Kim is a organizer. The day that I arrived at their front door, they were gettng delivery of 600 pounds of cat litter.

AMY

Do they have a cat now, or were they simply getting your room ready ? Here all I could offer you was a feathery bed.

MUFFIN

Clearly, you all mistake my observations for whining. Believe me, at a certain point in life, peals of complaint metamorphose into pearls of wisdom.

DAMON

Text me when you attain that elevated status.

AMY

I am through chatting. I have gardening to do. You might see if any of our men friends are free to gossip. (*exits*)

DAMON

I have work as well. I'll be in the downstairs office. If the world ends, just leave me alone down there. (*begins to exit*)

SAWYER

Dad, I have a question for your before Armagedon. (*exits with Damon. Kylie turns to exit to garden*)

MUFFIN

Kylie, do you have a few minutes ?

KYLIE

I need to speak with Amy.
MUFFIN

You are spending a lot of time with Amy.

KYLIE

She and I are working on a project ?

MUFFIN

For Sawyer's birthday ?

KYLIE

In a way. But, it may not be until next year's.

MUFFIN

Is that why you've been staying in the guest room ? You live just a few doors down. This must be one big birthday gift.

KYLIE

I hope so. We could text each other, but Amy prefers to have our conversations face to face.

MUFFIN

Let's talk once you have finished your project meetiing.
(*Kylie exits and Sawyer returns, mask in his shirt pocket*)

MUFFIN

What the heck is it with these masks?

SAWYER

Have you noticed that the virus originated in China, as do the masks. Is that relevant?

MUFFIN

No. I chalk it up to coincidence. What puzzles me is that you wear the same one for days at a time. If my dentist behaved similarly, I'd drop her like a used paper plate at a family a reunion.

SAWYER

We are family here, mostly.

MUFFIN

Sure we are Sawyer. But the group on your father's mother's side is a bit, well, they are just a bit special. It doesn't really matter. These masks are « disposable » but you've carry yours like some golden family heirloom to be displayed at every non special occasion. If it is a question of money, I will give you my Uncle Bill's handkerchieves. They haven't been sneezed into for years.

SAWYER

I appreciate that's, I guess.

MUFFIN

I can't very well give you a box of masks for your birthday, that would be an action by someone cheap and tacky.

Sawyer, I hope for your sake that you change your underwear more often than your mask. It's beginning to turn yellow.

Your father seems to be more upbeat today. His editor offered encouraging advice. Do you like to write ?

SAWYER

I don't know. Dad had me read Hamlet. He told me that I needed to read one Shakespeare, it likes taking the last childhood vaccine.

Maybe he believes that it is great literature or maybe he expected that being familiar with its well known quotes would help me prosper a world that no longer exists. It has vanished with Banquo's ghost.

MUFFIN

So you read two plays.

SAWYER

I got tired of staring at screens. Hamlet was a dufus, all he had to do was say nothing and his life would have been wonderful. You said the other day not to care too much.

MUFFIN

Did I say that ? Hmm. So why Macbeth ?

SAWYER

Because of the mirror and its presumed ghost. Mom takes it seriously, Dad ignores it, and I wanted to see what Shakespeare's opinion was. Plus, the play is short. It was silly talk, the ghost stuff that is. And then I read No Exit.

MUFFIN

Because of ghosts ?

SAWYER

Because of this confinement. Ghosts are silly. This farce call for an extra fool. The mirror phantom is too unreliable. I'm glad that you are here, Aunt Muffin. Not that you are a fool, just that we needed somebody. Openings remain for an idiot to be added, we have not yet exceeded out quota.

My mother acted in High School, sometimes I feel that she imagines herself still on stage. Being stuck inside can resemble a nonstop rehearsal where the dialogue is always similar but never identical.

Mom's message is simple, she is her own cult and as the only son, I should strive to emulate her. She provides examples on how to follow in her ferragamo footsteps and is disappointed when I don't. She is convinced that it is a a matter of insufficient willpower and intelligence on my part, and not one of having no desire to be like her.

I don't want to be in charge, but she doesn't cut it as role model.

MUFFIN

I will tell your about my own mother. She was so confident of her beliefs that she missed by a eyelashf getting her own chapter in the book of the world's religions. But, and this was strange, she made no effort to share her certitudes.

Her mothering responsibility ended in the delivery room. She would have made a good truck driver, to the unloading dock and not one step further.

And your father, Sawyer?

SAWYER

Dad is so wrapped up in plays, that he has his own religion as well, he is an apostle of the acts.

MUFFIN

Up until today, I believe that he was ready for Armageddon.

SAWYER

According to Googe newslinks, the end is two weeks away. Again. There are groups, that love the idea of the end of the world as we know it, it even has its own acronym so it must be popular. My dad is not one of those kooks. He enjoys it only it abstract, like a ghost story well told around a campfire. Ghosts and more ghosts.

MUFFIN

We will get through this.

SAWYER

The chicken littles won't be satisfied. They are going to wake up one day, disappointed to be alive without having killed any of their fellow humans.

MUFFIN

And what about you, grand nephew? Are you not totally bored with this pandemic? You're immune, or so they say. How do you like your forced emprisonnent? It's not like your self-imposed virtual world.

SAWYER

Shakespeare is poetic, Sartre is truthful I'm the untipped bell hop in No Exit, neglibile money and fewer lines.. I miss the fantasy of real life.

MUFFIN

Six words that summarize the past twenty years.

SAWYER

For you?

MUFFIN

Maybe, I was referring to the young, but, yes, you may be onto something there. Me too. I want to slow things down.

But here I am, rolling down the interstate, trying to exit, any exit will do, but each is less attractive than the preceding one, and the young bastards obliviously driving their priuses and Teslas won't let me change lanes. I see hanging from their mirrors these blue masks, dangling like some high school graduation tassel or hospital themed sex toy.

Holing up in a South Carolina beach house was only a prison transfer, a sliding glass door in lieu of bars, the din of bells replaced by the cry of seagulls, but still the same life sentence.

You do angst excellently, Aunt Muffin ! Don't look surprised. I'm familar with the definition of angst. I'm a mature teenager.

MUFFIN

Whereas I am a septanarian spring chicken. Does that make you suicidal ? Don't answer. If you are, just wait for a few more years, you'll outgrow it. And if not, well then self murder is appreciated better with age, like a French wine.

Look at me, I still have time to find a tall bridge if I need one. Unfortunately, all the ones in this town are toll bridges, and it bothers me to think of having paid a surcharge when I would not;t have crossed the entire span.

SAWYER

You could walk.
MUFFIN

You suggesting walking as if were a real possibility.

SAWYER

UBER ?
MUFFIN

Yet another four letter word uttered aloud before your elderly aunt. With a cab, there would still be a fee involved. Researching methods of suicide is analogous to preparing oneself to commit murder.

Do I strike you as the murdering type ?

SAWYER

Sometimes no, but usually yes.

MUFFIN

Suicide is such a ridiculous choice when you consider all the work involved. What to wear ? Should I leave the jewelry behind ?. It is easier to carry on with life, and let delegate Death the trivial details.

It was you who first mentioned angst. Are you full of angst ? Because if you are worried, I counsel you to jam all of it into one of your mothers's countless shoeboxes and to bury it deeply in a hole in the back yard. I'd even excavate it for you.

SAWYER

Would you ? I might be able to scrounge up some surplus worry from Dad. Would you truly take trowel in hand, plunging it repeatedly into the soil in the back yard ?

MUFFIN

Not me personally. I would pay to have it done. Those workers of Ernesto's appear quite handy with their tools. If you were to bury this cardboard container of concerns and return in 40 of 50 years, you would discover that both the box and its contents had faded away to nothingness.

Sawyer, do you have other girlfriends, other than Kylie ?

SAWYER

Girl friends of two words ?

MUFFIN

Of either variety.

SAWYER

I have friends who are girls, some here in Lake Forest. But they don't visit for fear of infecting their parents or grandparents. Its funny though, children don't have have parents and grandparents for being vulnerable. Maybe parents have children in an attempt to become invulnerable. Then they despise their offspring.

MUFFIN

You are wrong. The old don't hate the young. Well they do, a little, youth is envied, that is understandable. Your mother was born to hate, it is her nature. It becomes her. I can't picture her satisfied wearing any other color.

And by the way, you are not invulnerable to falling sick to this virus or of being human.

SAWYER

Aunt Muffin, what do you think of Kylie?

MUFFIN

What are my choices?

SAWYER

I don't understand

MUFFIN

It's your question

SAWYER

Yes, but it is not multiple choice, it is more fill in the blank.

MUFFIN

Kylie is not a blank. She is filled out, pretty well as you must have noticed.

SAWYER

You understand the question, Auntie.

MUFFIN

You call me Auntie when angry.

SAWYER

And you say I'm angry when I call you Auntie. What do you think of Kylie?

MUFFIN

A fill in the blank question, an essay then, with no horribly incorrect answer?

SAWYER

Yes.

MUFFIN

No hints?

SAWYER

Not one.

MUFFIN

Ok. My answer is that you are perfect for one another and that you should run away together, now, tonight, before events conspire to destroy your future before it has begun.

Go, live your lives in a fabulous, foreign resort, where you and Kylie can earn a livable salary by teaching English to the young children of drug dealers and corrupt politicians. You might even have your older students perform Hamlet.

SAWYER

Aunt Muffin, you amaze me. I did not expect such a flippant response.

MUFFIN

In other words you don't like it.

SAWYER

Well, you didn't actually answer the question.

MUFFIN

Of course with a hint, I might have done better.

SAWYER

How?

MUFFIN

For example, I might have replied that Kylie is a deliberate, manipulative dragon who will destroy any hope you possess of happiness and self fulfillment after the age of 2 Kylie is still a child, she still thinks of games as life. Her action is without plot, her violence lacks direction. But I have only met Kylie once.

SAWYER

Auntie!

MUFFIN

See, you are angry.

SAWYER

How can you speak of Kylie in those terms. It's insulting.

MUFFIN

So you prefer answer A, Sawyer? (*Pause*). I have only met your friend once, maybe twice. I know nothing about her. I am Auntie Muffin, not Uncle Sherlock.

You handed me a dart, spun me around a few times, and demanded that I pierce an invisible target.

SAWYER

Kylie is wonderful. You have spent time with her on many occasions. She has been over here numerous times. How many walks have we taken together ?

MUFFIN

A handful of brief encounters. The TSA agents at the airport can render as valid a judgmenton Kylie as i an able to do. They've seen the contents of her purse. That is one up on me. Go ask them, once Sandiford Field reopens.

MUFFIN

They renamed it to Muhammad Ali airport.

MUFFIN

Is Kylie your girlfriend, Sawyer?

SAWYER

Not in the way you mean it and I want it to be.

MUFFIN

She is hard.

SAWYER

Not to me.

MUFFIN

Not yet.

SAWYER

She is soft to me. Soft with me. (*Pause*). Kylie protects me with her tough shell.

MUFFIN

You're 17, you should have begun growing your own shell by now.

SAWYER

Kylie is.....we have an agreement.

MUFFIN

Is she aware of this agreement ? Will she keep to it ? Betrayal is a chess piece highly prized by elite players.

You are so calm, where is your emotion?

SAWYER

We protect each other.

MUFFIN

You protect her?

SAWYER

Yes.

MUFFIN
How? With your hard shell that I've not yet glimpsed these past weeks?

SAWYER

You are unobservant when it comes to other people, even your nearest relatives. We are not close relatives, no just near family. Within six feet of each other but it feels like more than six degrees of separation.

We are all separate, Sawyer. If it is truly to death us do part, why bury a deceased widow next to her late husband. Doesn't she have an out clause, based on time served?

My opinion is that Kylie is out of your league.

SAWYER

Shes like her were always out of my league.

MUFFIN

That is not what I meant, she is..

SAWYER

But that to is changing. Don't you understand, Aunt Muffin ? I am nearly grown, I can feel boyhood falling away like grime during a shower. I know to keep my hard shell covered with a pleasant, comforting blanket.

MUFFIN

You have an idealized view of life.

SAWYER

You have the ideal life.

MUFFIN

Not any longer. It comes to end an end when you reach one of the zero birthdays. It becomes less than perfect. The nonideal Death begins to buzz more loudly, like a hesitant bee approaching a past bloom flower. Its not as attractive as the image I implanted in your mind. You are a young bee, still potent. You think again of Kylie.

Death to the young is romantic, ironically you with perfect vision see him hazily, my failing eyes recognize him clearly. To you, abstract, with me he is as flesh and blood as myself, possibly more so.

SAWYER

So I should carpe diem ?

MUFFIN

Sieze the day is BS advice. There is no alternative, it is the only advice. Its like telling people to breath, to eat. Seriously, you need to be told that ? Whatever choice you make in your life, you live to regret. If you live long enough, you will learn to regret nothing.

SAWYER

I'm not too young to have plans.

MUFFIN

How far into the future due these plans extend? A week, a month?

SAWYER

I admit that my plans are short term.

MUFFIN

Nature is unkind to young men. It's a choice of sex or war, and one has gone out of fashion.
Lately, I've been thinking
MUFFIN

What have you been thinking, Sawyer?

SAWYER

That COVID may have come now when it did for a reason. And (*pause*)

MUFFIN

For which reason?

SAWYER

That maybe we need a change.

MUFFIN

We? Or you?

SAWYER

Me. I need a change. You agree with me. I'm right, aren't I?

MUFFIN

My wrinkles say no. they also tell me that you invisible shell is being to show. Bravo.

SAWYER

I like the mask, it's

MUFFIN

Erotic? Seductive. Don't blush Sawyer. I was young once too. A century or so ago. I remember, everything was seductive back then. I can see that I'm right. Embarrassent doesn't hide truth, it confirms it. Everything is a bauble, Sawyer, women doubly so. Women love and like being baubles.

SAWYER

Thanks for the talk Aunt Muffin, is was fun. I didn't expect it to be so. And informative. But..

MUFFIN

But what ?

SAWYER

Don't consider this discussion as a way to avoid getting me a birthday gift. Men like baubles, too. (*exits*)

MUFFIN

Kylie is already a hard woman, she had the benefit of the best education that the internet and the real world provide for free. Yet she is fluent in the language of words both spoken and unspoken. Damn that mirror. A perfect guest would smash it.

(*Kylie enters*)

KYLIE

Hi Muffin, we're all through in the garden. What did you
want to discuss ?

MUFFIN

Nothing in particular. Life in general.

KYLIE

Sure, why not.

MUFFIN

Your hands are spotless. Did you wear gloves? Or is hand
sanitizer required in the garden ?

KYLIE

Neither. Amy declines an ally in the battle against weeds. She
enjoys doing the dirty parts herself. I prefer to keep my fingers
clean, so it works out well.

MUFFIN

You must need clean hands to use a smartphone. Would you
wager that Sawer or Damon is on his more ? They study the
screen as if it holds the keys to a kingdom instead of being another

KYLIE

It's invaluable, a never expiring ticket to the world. Don't you have one ?

MUFFIN

Its around somewhere. To be honest, it is overwhelming. I can't keep up with the expanding universe that you hold so casually in your hand. Do you and Sawyer text a lot ?

KYLIE

Probably a lot by your measure.

MUFFIN

You don't spend much time together.

KYLIE

We are rehearsing for the perfect marriage. Seriously, Sawyer is a minor, for a few more hours. Maybe we will be closer afterwards. What we have works for us.
Let me ask you a question, don't laugh.
Do you think that men are born with menopause ? They reach puberty and they continue to whine and complain.

MUFFIN

If you include Sawyer in that category, I am confident that you are in for a pleasant surprise.

KYLIE

Really ?

MUFFIN

Yes, really.

KYLIE

Amy told me that you have traveled extensively, using taking a home and not making a home.

MUFFIN

Guilty as charged. Its like an ocular migrane, where I lose peripherial vision. As someone who has lived the bulk of my existence on the periphery, I don't relish the thought of forced confinement. I bring as well as I take. Amy has her own blindspot when it comes to me.

KYLIE

You're telling me. This pandemic is worse than repeating sophomore high school. I'm not permitted to do anything worth doing. Here I am, stuck at home and the future will be as boring as far I can visualize it.

Just like sophomore year. I tell myself every morning and every evening that junior year is a day closer. I enjoyed those twelve months, but I've almost convinced myself that the twelve months after this virus is dead will be twice as exhilarating.

This new normal is a defective dream. In a dream you can do anything. Now,I wake and rediscover that you I can't do anything.

MUFFIN

Kylie, that is exactly how I used to think, about the old normal. Normal is for normal people. Is that what you are ? (*pause, no response*). I didn't think so.

But, oh, I don't really understand, but it suddenly seemed that if I dreamed hard enough it became reality

KYLIE

That is delusion.

MUFFIN

Maybe, but I like it.

KYLIE

Or insanity.

MUFFIN

Delusional and insane are mark down stickers attached to women like (*pause*). I've learned not to care what other people think, they are nothing more than shadows in dreams ignored.

KYLIE

The people or the dreams?

MUFFIN

Both. It was so much easier once I realized that these shadows had never cared about me. Except when I behaved badly, in their opinion.

KYLIE

That's natural. They term it societal norms.

MUFFIN

No, it's envy. And I am not responsible for or obliged to sooth their petty envies. I freed myself from their constraints as well as my own.

It was foolish to persevere in assigning them any power in my life. We each have our own separate nocturnal dreams, why not continue that distinction while the sun was up ?

KYLIE

I'm 20 now. How old are you, again?

MUFFIN

Too old to remember 20. Can you credit it, Kylie, this is still my first life ? I'm a reincarnation virgin, not a reincarnated one. There is a qualitative difference. Given how it has gone so far, I will probably just ask for the check afterwards and call it a permanent good night, rather than ask for another ride.

How old am I now?

KYLIE

Yeah, that is what I meant to ask

MUFFIN

You should know better than to ask me that.. My late husband liked to depress others, including me. In that he was master.

KYLIE

Sorry.

MUFFIN

I was worried about Sawyer.

KYLIE

He's hormonal. All men are.

MUFFIN

Young men are attracted to the women in their seductive masks.

KYLIE

Of course he is. Sawyer finds anything and everything about women attractive and seductive. If they twitch that renders him fool and them approachable. Two consecutive shivers and that is an open invitation in his eyes. It's like a story from Arabian Nights.

MUFFIN

Have you read it?

KYLIE

Of course not.

MUFFIN

You are hard.

KYLIE

Thank you.

MUFFIN

Even for a woman.

KYLIE

Thanks, I know that. I am proud my hardness. Men can be such..

MUFFIN

Wimps ?

KYLIE

Non men. I swear, if men were still manly they would outlaw sports and revitalize war. Sunday afternoon television would be watchable again. This is not how I envisioned my gap year.

MUFFIN

Home life is extraordinarily crowded. At the same time, you must be learning things about you and the rest of the world that are new and exciting.

KYLIE

New? Maybe. Exciting, no. But Amy has an idea....

MUFFIN

What idea is that?

KYLIE

I'm sorry, but we can't discuss it.

MUFFIN

A secret?

KYLIE

Yes.

MUFFIN

That is exciting. It's been a while since I've been part of a good secret, being on the outside of it is disappointing, but simply being aware that you and Amy are participating in one let's me enjoy it vicariously. That is some consolation.

Perhaps you and I can create another one for us.

KYLIE

I'm not sure

MUFFIN

I understand. I'll see if Damon are Sawyer are game for some clandestine activity.

KYLIE

Still, I'd much rather have had a gap year overseas than, than this. Here is to next year, may it be if not wonderful, then not this. I may be hopeful or delusional, or is that the same condition?

MUFFIN

You may be an exception.

KYLIE

What happens here in virusland..

MUFFIN

Stays in virusland?

KYLIE

Nope. We post it on social media. It won't be a cure but it should cause some chuckles. I'd like to feel the world shake with laughter.

I fear that soon, I won't be able to look at an unmasked man in public. It's another unforeseen consequence of this pandemic, do you think it might become a fetish? I do.

MUFFIN

I don't know..

KYLIE

A fetish requiring high priced therapy.

MUFFIN

That sounds like an unlikely bug to catch, no pun intended. At the same time this is somewhat fun. The novelty and the unknown is compelling. Apart from a few people dying, this is kinda fun.

KYLIE

Kinda fun ? It's just that this is the nearest to catastrophe that the average American has been in his sheltered life. They panic and worse, they relish the panic. The panic grows because they blithely feed it every two hours, like some monstrous baby in a long forgotten fairy tale.

MUFFIN

Its an adventure.

KYLIE

Or death.

MUFFIN

There is always death. Its either death with adventure or death without adventure. I prefer my salad fully loaded.

KYLIE

You make it sound like dining at Eddie Merlot's.

MUFFIN

There are worse restaurants. Bill always liked it. One thing he was skilled at was using flatware.

KYLIE

They were going to die anyway. Is that what you are saying ?

MUFFIN

We all die.
The other day I went for a drive, not far, just around Middletown. It was a warm day. I was sitting at the traffic light coming out of Kroger's parking lot.

KYLIE

Isn't that encroaching on Damon's turf ?

MUFFIN

We won't tell him this particular story then. That traffic light is so long and i put down my driver's window. I heard the sound of traffic passing back and forth in front of me, the hum and roar of engines and rubber on concrete.

KYLIE

Krogers is the place to be nowadays.

MUFFIN

The metronone of the turn signal accompanied the Sirius/XM radio playing an artist that you've never heard of. On my bare knee I felt the gentle movement of air conditioned to coldness, while bright sunlight streamed through the clean windshield.

I was grateful to the unkown traffic engineer who had designed such an impossibly long red. It was a glorius 20th century moment in the 21st, one that I could have prolonged indefinitely. It was my own private performance art masterpiece.

KYLIE

You make waiting for a green light such a tranquil experience. I don't have that level of patience.

MUFFIN

It was tranquility iself, but I also remember thinking, if COVID tried to traverse the crosswalk that lay before me, I would so plaster his ass.

But, like all things that must pass, this peaceful moment likewise passed. With regret.

This virus too will pass, and will be soon forgotten and looked back on in distant years with a kind of machocistic nostalgia.

KYLIE

Like the multiple dead in auto accidents can't prevent the allure of the open road.

Muffin, this virus is more real to you than it is to me. It's an abstract danger, like being smacked by lightning, fatal yes, but unlikely to individually fry me. And yet, you seem to ignore it.

MUFFIN

I have so many bacterial enemies that I fear none of them inordinately. Three years ago, I passed a week in the woods in a concrete block cabin from the 1920s. It has survived what nature and inattentive campers did to it. It lacked electricity and running water. The scent of wood smoke lingered in my clothes for days after my stay as a not undesirable companion. I survived.

I read Shakespeare, he was a wonderful poet but a poor historians. His facts were not the reality of the scholar, but it is he we believe.

KYLIE

Is he the sixteenth centry version of internet reality ?

MUFFIN

Apparently so. He demonstrated that we are entitled to our private, now public opinions.

KYLIE

But not our own facts.

MUFFIN

You are a twenty first century woman. You and I can converse in nearly the same language. You are not naive. I see now that you are Sawyer are a team, perfect for life's stage.

The man who said that we are not entitled to our own facts is now dead, and his truth, such as it never was, died with him. I stand by my truth, and I am alive.

KYLIE

You isolated yourself in a cottage in the words . Why ? To preserve yourself ? Never mind. I don't want an answer. Its not important.
Now, here you are three years later. What have you learned about yourself? Other than needing other people?

MUFFIN

Some people more than others.I learned that is impossible to get a hairdresser to make a cabin call. So, I returned to civilization..

COVID is the least competent of assassins. Death must be slipping.

KYLIE

I find that very unlikely, Muffin.

MUFFIN

He is too sensitive in my opinion. They claim that sunlight will kill it rapidly.

And me, much more slowly. This Kentucky sun is burns at half brilliance, you should experience it at full power in South Carolina. The difference is like that between Death and his cousin, Infirmity. Age is cruel, sadistic, thoroughly prepatory in design. I much prefer the kindess of Death.
The concerns of the young are no longer mine, I've left them behind like the old neighborhoods that I moved from.

KYLIE

And who are the young ?

MUFFIN

I'm generous. Young includes those still working.

KYLIE

For real or for Gemerel Mills?

MUFFIN

I've lived an adventurous life. I pity young people today. Their adventures are secondhand, virtual. For every real person, there are thousands of voyeurs, followers they call themselves, without any hint of shame. Its undignified.

Consider the thousand lives not well lived, for every one lived in a such a ridiculous manner. We are either encouraged to create our own hoaxes, and failing that lazily, to believe wholeheartedly the imaginings of others.

You are worth more than simply an observer on another's life.

KYLIE

Do you place me among these vampires, Aunt Muffin ?

MUFFIN

That is a question for you yourself to answer. And whatever answer you tell yourself, it doesn't need to be the same response tomorrow. You are still cocooned, you must murder your caterpillar to take wing and flourish as a butterfly..

How went the project meeting?

KYLIE

It is still a secret. I can tell you that I toy with computer games. They are variations on one theme, violence. When worlds collide, it is better to be destructive than accomodating.

Find a team, destroy the enemy, and then find a better team. It is the lesson fo sports and business extended to cyberspace.

Collateral damage no longer deserves a footnote, losers are invisible and forgotten. Toleration is a necessary tactic while the plotting continues. The idea of a win/win is a consololation prize dreamed up by losers.

In brief, I create good, clean, satisfying mayhem.

MUFFIN

I see, I think. So you convert all this pleasant destruction into games that millions of people want to buy ?

KYLIE

Yes. We are all capitalists, from the first monkey who didn't want to share, to you and I.

But it is make believe. This is a game, nothing more than make believe. Yes, make believe as a business. Players may even return in another life. In this world, reincarnation is taken for granted. See, its all good.

MUFFIN

Your endeavor is fearsome, it sounds like these games could serve as simulations, reherasals for violence in the non cyber world.

KYLIE

I could only be that lucky.

MUFFIN

The situation is drastic. I must act likewise. I need drastic, a double, straight up, forget the ice. (*goes and pours herself a bourbon*)

Kylie, truth is like a grenade. You must toss it, damn the consequences. If you don't you end up hurting yourself. Throw the damn thing and hope for the best.

Come approach, I will tell you my secrets, a few at least, among them my age. (*Kylie approaches*)

(*Leans and whispers in Kylie's ear. Takes longer than expected*)

Enjoy the ride and the jealousy. They warn that jealousy has a bitter taste, but I always found it on the sweet side. So enjoy your current ride if you prefer it to the new model that I've found for you. This current adventure will be over too soon enough.

KYLIE

Too soon enough? What does that even mean? (*Muffin shrugs, Kylie exits*)

MUFFIN

I regard the person in the mirror, the one behind my own reflection. But there is no one, certainly not Amy's phantom. More accurate to picture the spectre of Amy.

No, I observe solely my own fears and hopes. As to glimpse them, a looking glass is not required.

Those who believe in nothing are bigger fools than those who give credence to the weirdest of fantasies. (*finishes drink, but continues to hold it*)

I detect the stench of conspiracy, it is vague in detail but overpowering in goal My welcome, such as it ever was, is in tatters. I must collect and leave this ex-home.

By my reckoning, I am owed three cans of tuna, large, white, and packed in water. The two of us, the fish and I perfectly mismatched as travel companions. He packed and in water, as to me my suitcase stays undone, myself clearly out of comfortable depths.

What else? By rights, I claim in addition a pair of Charmin rolls, not yet dampened.

Discretion is the better part of valor, daily life for women. II will leave. Not tonight, for I fear driving in darkness more than whatever threat may approach under its cover.

One more night under the shelter of my loving family, my door securely bolted. (*places empty bourbon glass underneath mirror and exits*)

AMY

(*late at night, little illumination, enters carrying a covered tray*)

This is a perfect end to a perfect day, with more than perfect to arrive tomorrow. It was Spring, and Summer, and Winter's holiday in 12 hours.

The warm rain was marvelous, it blossomed the intoxicating vapor delivered by a summer shower, a natural scent that cannot be countefeited. It promised all that lays beyon COVID and now beyond Muffin.

Muffin could have contributed more, but no, that is not her way. It's not really murder, when it is self defense.

Youth is wasted on the young as in death on the aged. Neither merit it. But Muffin is the exception that proves the rule. (*sets tray down on table next to empty bourbon glass*)

It's so exhilarating to realize that laws are only for little people. It's pure freedom, more intoxicating than any spirit, bourbon or otherwise. (*picks up glass, smells its remnants and sets it down again*)

I need to strike before I die. Its a long time hunger not yet satisfied. If not my husband who is beyond ripe and now unpleasantly scents the house, and not my dear son, and surely not my talented but oblivous accomplice, who could ask for better assistance, then it falls to the sole remaining contestant.

And tonight recalls Christmas Eves past, milk and cookies laid the night before..

But our next visitor will not be Santa but Death who must content himself with a rich, unpleasant tasting offering in the form of a Muffin crumpled. This cake, doctored by a nurse will be ear Auntie's last (*picks up boubon glass again and exits*)

DAMON
(*enters a few seconds later*)

Amy is practical, but then most women are practical. She doesn't understand how I think, but she knows perfectly well what I require. In summary, she is a perfect wife and an excellent warder.

Doris was explicit, it is preferrable to murder than it is to starve. I will practice my own escape tonight, one of these baked goods needs some simple spice. (*sprinkles something on one of the muffins, exits*)

KYLIE
(*enters a few seconds later, carrying a cake decorator and paper towels*)

This task would be child's play online. Instead, my sweat is real, my fear is genuine, and the rapidity of my young heart drums in my ears. If I were not well raised, I would take Sawyer tonight while he is but yet a boy. Twelve hours will only render me more ravenous and he more amazed.

I will content myself with work. It would be simpler to trash this tray of Amy's handiwork, but that would delay the game. (*Does something to muffins and exits*)

DAMON
(*Damon on stage with Kylie and Sawyer, in black mourning*)
(*Directed to a person offstage*)

Now that she is gone, do you miss her ? (*recurring sound as Muffin wears sneakers and Amy is always in loud heels*)

(*Sound of approaching heels, then Muffin enters*)?

MUFFIN

Of course I do, Damon.

DAMON

It was a lovely service, but I'd have expected a bigger turnout.

MUFFIN

It was because of the virus, people are aftraid of death in the best of times, and these are not the best of times.

DAMON

I feel bad.

MUFFIN

Of course you do. We all feel bad, more or less

DAMON

That isn't what I feel bad about, not the only thing. Take that mirror for instance. She was so enamored with it. She spoke of it and to it as if it were some ancient, mystical crystal that aided her in dealing with this epidemic.

KYLIE

She loved that mirror. It was her one and only antique. From the 16th century she liked to say.

DAMON

Sawyer, do you remember a month or so ago, when you and your mother went to visit Aunt Shelia in Corbin ? You were gone for a day or so. It was after the mirror was installed.

SAWYER

Sure, Dad. It was our last trip before everything closed. We should have gone to Disneyworld instead.

DAMON

Well, the first night, the mirror fell from the wall. It didn't shatter into a million pieces, but it was smashed nevertheless.

KYLIE

What did you do ? Did you have it repaired ?

DAMON

It was beyond salvageable. I had the glass replaced, the frame wa dimpeled in one spot. A three or four centuries, what is one more dent ?

MUFFIN

Which means that this magical glass is just glass.

DAMON

It is a mirror, a simple mirror. It works as well as any other looking glass. Amy was just as beautiful and just as comforted by it as one of 300 years.

There is more.

The night before she died, I sprinkled salt on the icing of Amy's muffin. It was devious, but I was worried since she had complained about losing her sense of taste. Remember, Sawyer ? They claim that can be a side effect of this virus. It was just salt, not poison.

SAWYER

The doctor said that mom died from a heart attack, Dad. Was she wrong?

DAMON

No. I don't know, maybe. But you were there Sawyer. Your mother didn't notice the salt flavor. Aunt Muffin and Kylie did Amy mention hers tasting odd?

KYLIE

I don't recall her saying anything to that effect.

DAMON

So it might be that the virus claimed another victim.

MUFFIN

I don't want to appear cruel, but does it matter how she died? It was quick and any suffering was brief. The service was beautiful, Amy would have been so pleased that the entire congregation was masked.

DAMON

All nine of us?

MUFFIN

There were many more there in spirit, Damon. And I remain here myself only in spirit. This is as good a time as any. With the three three of you here, I can bid adieu once.

I'm leaving to visit cousin Trudy in Pennsylvania. Her farm can be bleak, but at this time of year, it is gorgeous. I need gorgeous. Damon, you should come along.

DAMON

I can't, not now.

DAMON

Then soon. You can write in solitude.

SAWYER

Or write of solitude, Dad. I could come along and make sure that whatever you write you don't veer into Hamlet. One of those is enough.

DAMON

Maybe. I have your phone number. (*leaves then turns and continues to exit*)

Check with Trudy. If there is room, and if its not an imposition, then call me. Sawyer and I will drive up. Hmm, General Mills, a real General Mills cookie. (*Takes one from the box, begins to exits, then returns and takes the entire box, exits*)

SAWYER

Aunt Muffin ? Before you give Dad the greenlight, make sure that they have internet, and (*pause*) we will both need a set of essential worker papers. Give Dad an impressive title, but I'm ok with being his assistant.

MUFFIN

That's good, Sawyer, as he will need your assistance for quite a while.

SAWYER

And maybe one for Kylie ?

KYLIE

Not right away Sawyer. You and your dad need to be alone, with family, and I am not family yet.

MUFFIN

Besides, Kylie has a job now, here.

KYLIE

Yes, its a game, like Fornite, that I've been working on, with you mother. I approached Muffin about it, and she was very enthustiastic.

MUFFIN

Enthuiastic and supportive. I've become an investor. Kylie was even able to complete some testing early, just a few days ago. Oh, what do you call it ?

KYLIE

Alpha testing. That was successful. This is going to be a killer app.

MUFFIN

But now, I'd just be in the way, dead wood so to speak. Kylie can focus on her priorities, and you and your dad can concentrate on yours. In three months, who knows ? And Sawyer, I already checked, they have high speed internet, and here are papers for you and Damon. I'll call in two days to give Damon the greenlight, he will be ready then. In the interim, don't say anything, but you may want to start packing.

SAWYER

This is awesome. Thanks Aunt Muffin. In three months, I will have caught up to you Kylie.

KYLIE

I say more like three weeks. (*kisses Sawyer who then exits*)

Now that she is gone, will you miss Amy?

MUFFIN

Yes, for a while. But I will miss her only because she missed me. I am going to miss him.

KYLIE

Him ?

KYLIE

Why is COVID a him ?

MUFFIN

He is casual in his brutality. He is not calculating like women can be, especially young women. (*pause*) No matter.

We never met, we had no heated relationship that could exhaust itself into dislike.

As for Amy, she left no impact on me, no not in that way. She left no impression, while COVID did. I won't forget him soon, if at all.

KYLIE

The virus is still out there.

MUFFIN

True, but I sense that he has had fling with me, months ago. I'll get tested one of these days. But he has left, as all of my men have left. It was romantic while it lasted. Well, maybe not romantic, that is too far. It was exciting.

KYLIE

Like war ?

MUFFIN

I've not known war. Maybe war as I pictured it at the home front, away from the gunfire, but still surrounded by the injured and reminded constantly of the dead.
Still, it wasn't quite real, it felt somehow dreamlike, vaporous, it was danger, but danger not first hand. These past hours, days, weeks, it was somewhere between listening to a ghost story and being vaporized by a bolt of lightning.
(*A rolling clap of thunder is heard in the distance*)
Yes, like that. At least it didn't storm during the funeral service.

In any event, it was as real as I'm willing to tolerate. Up to this point, I've successfully avoided real life, as carefully as most people avoid real death.

KYLIE

And you regret that ?

MUFFIN

(*Muffin removes heels and puts on her mules*)
Hell no. I regret that its coming to an end. You and I, we like our games, but only our games. I'm getting too old to play my own, but

I'm pleased to see you begin yours. Look around, you might ask Damon if he would you like you to stay here during his absence, this palace needs a new queen, and you are perfect in that role.

Kylie, the icing on my cupcake was salty.

KYLIE

Was it ? Mine tasted fine, it was delicious.

MUFFIN

And the letter M was smeared, it looked like a redone A

KYLIE

Damon must be repsonsible.

MUFFIN

When he sprinkled the salt?

KYLIE

Yes, that explains it.

MUFFIN

Yes, I guess that explains it. (*Muffin exits*)

KYLIE

(*removes her own shoes and puts on the heels and regards herself in the mirror*) It begins. A new day, a new mirror, and a new queen.

FIN